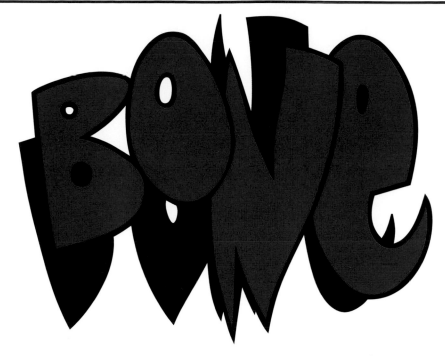

THE ADVENTURE BEGINS

BY JEFF SMITH

WITH COLOUR BY STEVE HAMAKER

Scholastic Canada Ltd.

Toronto New York London Auckland Sydney
Mexico City New Delhi Hong Kong Buenos Aires

Scholastic Canada Ltd.
604 King Street West, Toronto, Ontario M5V 1E1, Canada

Scholastic Inc.
557 Broadway, New York, NY 10012, USA

Scholastic Australia Pty Limited
PO Box 579, Gosford, NSW 2250, Australia

Scholastic New Zealand Limited
Private Bag 94407, Botany, Manukau 2163, New Zealand

Scholastic Children's Books
Euston House, 24 Eversholt Street, London NW1 1DB, UK

Library and Archives Canada Cataloguing in Publication

Smith, Jeff, 1960 Feb 27-
     The adventure begins / Jeff Smith.

(Bone)
Contents: 1. Out From Boneville -- 2. The great cow race -- 3. Eyes of
the storm ISBN 978-1-4431-0480-7

     I. Title.   II. Series: Smith, Jeff, 1960 Feb. 27- . Bone.

PN6727.S546A68 2010   741.5'973   C2010-903222-5

ACKNOWLEDGMENTS
Harvestar Family Crest designed by Charles Vess
Map of The Valley by Mark Crilley
Color by Steve Hamaker

Book design by David Saylor

6 5 4 3 2 1   Printed in Singapore 46   10 11 12 13 14

CONTENTS

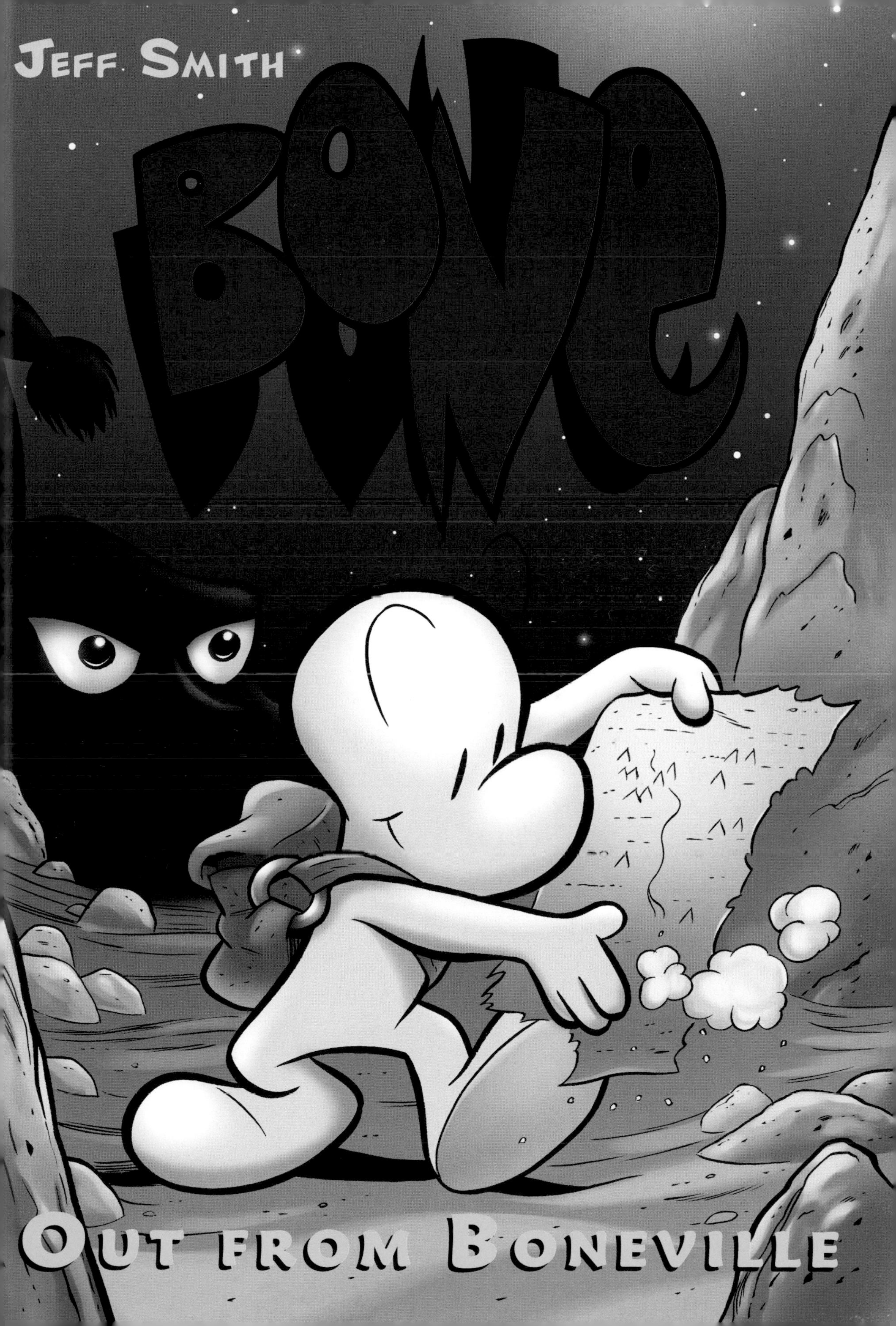
JEFF SMITH
BONE
OUT FROM BONEVILLE

This book is for Vijaya

DON'T GET HIM STARTED.

THEY CAN'T **DO** THIS TO **ME!** YOU CAN'T DO ANYTHING TO A **RICH** PERSON THAT HE DOESN'T **WANT!**

GASP! OH! TH' HORRIBLE INJUSTICE OF IT ALL! I'M STILL **REELING** WITH **SHOCK!!**

I'M A RESPECTED COMMUNITY **LEADER!** A **SHINING PILLAR** OF **MORAL STRENGTH!**

... SO A COUPLE OF SHADY **BUSINESS** DEALS WENT SOUR... IS **THAT** ANY REASON TO RUN TH' MOST **BELOVED BONE** IN BONEVILLE OUT ON A **RAIL?!**

YES.

BELOVED? TH' MAYOR DECLARED A SCHOOL **HOLIDAY** JUST SO TH' KIDS COULD COME AND THROW **ROCKS** AT YOU!

INGRATES!

OH, THEY'LL **RUE** TH' DAY THEY CHASED **PHONCIBLE P. BONE** OUTTA THEIR CRUMMY OL' TOWN!

SNIFF!

NOW, NOW, LITTLE BUCKAROO! DON'T BE **SAD!** IT'S A BEAUTIFUL DAY! THERE'S NOT A **CLOUD IN TH' SKY!**

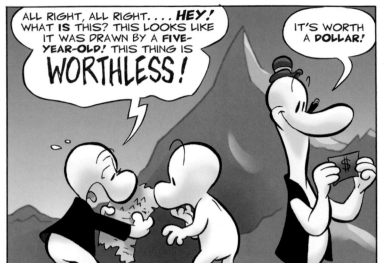

YEEEE! I CAN'T **BELIEVE I** WASN'T JUST **KILLED!**

PHONEY! SMILEY! GO BACK! DON'T COME THIS WAY! IT'S A CLIFF!

...MAYBE THEY'RE ALREADY DOWN HERE!

PHONEY BONE! SMILEY!

HEY! HEY, GUYS! I'M DOWN IN THIS GULLEY! CAN YOU HEAR ME?!!

HUH
HUH
HUH

HUFF!

WHERE TH' HECK **ARE** THOSE GUYS? WE'RE GOIN' STRAIGHT INTO TH' MOUNTAINS!

I HOPE I CATCH UP TO 'EM BEFORE IT GETS DARK . . . .

THE **LAST** THING I WANT TO DO IS SPEND THE NIGHT OUT HERE BY MYSELF!

. . . OF COURSE, AFTER A DAY LIKE **TODAY**, IT'S HARD TO IMAGINE THAT ANYTHING **WORSE** COULD HAPPEN . . .

YAWN!

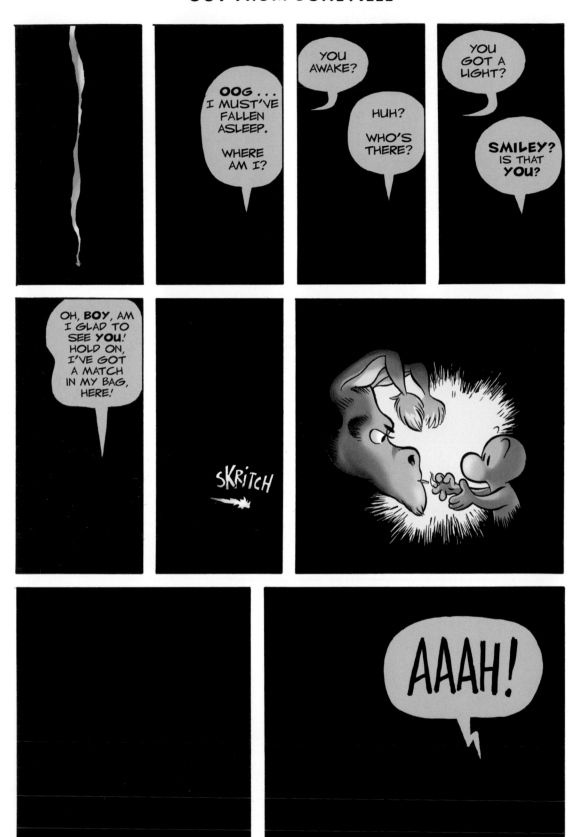

OH, **MAN**! THIS AIN'T GONNA **CUT IT**!

I ACTUALLY THOUGHT THIS MAP WOULD TAKE ME THROUGH TH' MOUNTAINS TO THIS WATERFALL ON HERE . . .

. . . BUT IF THIS THING WERE **REAL**, I WOULD'VE COME TO TH' PASS BY **NOW**! **ERRR**! I'M SO **STUPID**! I BET THIS MAP WAS JUST ONE OF SMILEY'S **PRANKS** – – AND I **FELL** FOR IT!

AND TO TOP IT **OFF**, I HAVEN'T SEEN ANY MORE **CIGAR BUTTS** ALL DAY . . . **HOW** DO I GET MYSELF **INTO** THESE THINGS?

OH, WELL . . . I'LL FIND THOSE GUYS **SOONER** OR LATER . . . **IF** I DON'T DIE OF THIRST . . .

UNTIL **THEN**, I JUST GOTTA KEEP MOVIN'! KEEP . . .

COOL.

I MADE IT!

THAT STUPID MAP WAS **RIGHT!** YESSIREE, **BOB!** THERE'S WATER ON TH' MENU **TONIGHT!**

I COULD **KISS** SMILEY BONE FOR FINDING THAT MAP!

I MIGHT EVEN KISS **PHONEY** RIGHT BEFORE I STRANGLE HIM!

AND LOOK! ONE OF SMILEY'S **CIGAR STUBS!**

HEY! WATCH IT! YOU ALMOST STEPPED ON ME!

WHOOPS! HELLO! WHAT ARE **YOU** SUPPOSED TO BE?

I'M TED! I'M A BUG!

YOU LOOK MORE LIKE A **LEAF!**

A **LEAF**?! THAT'S A **INSULT!** WHERE'S MY BIG BROTHER?

HEY, HOLD ON! I DIDN'T MEAN ANY HARM! BESIDES, WHAT COULD **YOUR** BIG BROTHER DO TO ME?

WHOA.

IS YOU PICKIN' ON TED?

I — JUST SAID HE LOOKS LIKE A LEAF!

WHAT ARE YOU? A TROUBLE-MAKER? WE DON'T NEED YOUR KIND IN OUR VALLEY!

I GUESS HE DIDN'T MEAN NO HARM, BIG BROTHER! YOU DON'T HAS TO HIT HIM IF YOU DON'T WANT!

LISTEN TO HIM! LISTEN TO HIM!

WELL, OKAY, TED, IF YOU SAY SO....

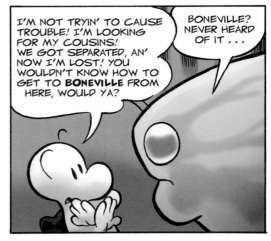

I'M NOT TRYIN' TO CAUSE TROUBLE! I'M LOOKING FOR MY COUSINS! WE GOT SEPARATED, AN' NOW I'M LOST! YOU WOULDN'T KNOW HOW TO GET TO **BONEVILLE** FROM HERE, WOULD YA?

BONEVILLE? NEVER HEARD OF IT...

BUT YOU BETTER FIND IT -- **FAST!** IT'S AUTUMN NOW, AN' WINTER STRIKES **QUICK** IN THESE PARTS... AN' WHEN IT DOES, **NOBODY** CAN GET THROUGH THOSE MOUNTAINS...

... IN **OR** OUT!

SO I SUGGEST YOU MAKE YOUR VISIT HERE A **SHORT** ONE, OR YOU'LL BE STUCK FOR TH' WINTER. AN' I DON'T THINK YOU WANNA **DO** THAT!

NO. DEFINITELY NOT.

GOOD. I'LL LET YA GO FOR **NOW**, SINCE TED SEEMS TO LIKE YA OKAY... BUT DON'T FERGET!

NO DAWDLIN'!

THANK YOU FOR NOT HITTING ME.

DON'T WORRY 'BOUT HIM... HE'S ACTUAL A REAL NICE GUY!

WELL... NOW WE GOTTA FIGGER OUT WHAT TA **DO** WITH YA... SAY! I KNOW! I'LL TAKE YA TO SEE THORN! C'MON! WHAT'S YER **NAME**, MISTER?

FONE BONE. SO WHO'S THIS THORN? HE'S NOT ANOTHER **BIG BUG**, IS HE?

HO, HO! **NO!** THORN KNOWS JES' ABOUT EVER'THIN' IN TH' **WHOLE WORLD!**

BUT, LISTEN, BONE! BIG BROTHER WAS RIGHT ABOUT WINTER! SHE HITS **FAST!** 'N' IF YOU WANTS TA GIT HOME, YOU GOTTA DO IT BEFORE SHE **SNOWS!**

DON'T WORRY! I'M JUST GONNA FIND MY COUSINS, AN' THEN I'M **OUTTA HERE!**

TED! WAIT FOR ME!

WELL, WELL... LOOK WHO'S JOINED US FOR SUPPER... GO START THE COOKING FIRE!!

NO. YOU CALLED ME FAT.

NO?!! WHAT DO YOU MEAN NO?!!

AND IT'S NOT THE FIRST TIME YOU'VE DONE IT, EITHER...

COMRADE... BE REASONABLE! I WASN'T THINKING--- I WAS TRYING TO CATCH OUR DINNER--- **THIS ISN'T THE TIME**---

I TAKE IT BACK.... YOU'RE NOT FAT.

TOO LATE!

PLEASE, COMRADE! I JUST WANT TO CHOP HIM UP FOR THE STEW!

AND THAT'S ANOTHER THING! I'M TIRED OF STEW! I WANT TO PUT HIM IN A CRUST AND BAKE A LIGHT FLUFFY QUICHE!

QUICHE?! WHAT KIND OF FOOD IS **THAT** FOR A MONSTER TO EAT?!...... LISTEN, DO YOU THINK YOU COULD COME BACK IN HALF AN HOUR? WE'LL HAVE THIS STRAIGHTENED OUT BY THEN!

WHY DIDN'T YOU STOP ME?

WHY **SHOULD** I? YOU'RE SO **SMART!**

HELLO, MIZ 'POSSUM! I HAVEN'T SEEN **YOU** IN A COUPLE OF MONTHS!

OH, I DON'T GET OUT OF TH' HOUSE MUCH IN **WINTER** 'SPECIALLY WITH **YOUNGUNS!**

THESE CAN'T BE **YOUR** KIDS! THEY'RE ALL GROWN UP!

WELL, IT'S ALMOST **SPRING!** THEY SHOOT UP **FAST** THIS TIME OF YEAR! YOU BOYS REMEMBER FONE BONE?

SURE!

YEAH!

HOW YOU GUYS DOIN'?

WE'RE COOL!

WHERE'D YA GET TH' **HAT?**

YOUR MOM MADE IT FOR ME!

PRETTY DORKY!

MOM BROUGHT YA SOME MORE **BLANKETS** 'N' STUFF!

WOW! THANKS! I DON'T KNOW **HOW** I WOULD'VE MADE IT THROUGH TH' WINTER WITHOUT YOU, MIZ 'POSSUM!

DON'T YOU **WORRY** ABOUT IT! AS LONG AS YOU'RE STUCK HERE IN OUR VALLEY, **I'LL** TAKE CARE OF YOU! HERE! I PACKED A PIE IN CASE YOU'RE HUNGRY!

DID YOU EVER FIND THOSE COUSINS OF YOURS?

NO, NOT YET. HAVE YOU SEEN **TED** SINCE I TALKED TO YOU LAST?

NOPE. DON'T KNOW MUCH ABOUT WHAT BUGS **DO** IN TH' WINTER, BUT I HAVEN'T SEEN WING **NOR** ANTENNAE OF TED SINCE TH' **SNOW** HIT...

SAY... WASN'T THERE SOMEONE **ELSE** YOU WANTED ME TO FIND OUT ABOUT?

TED WAS GONNA TAKE ME TO SEE SOMEONE NAMED **THORN.**

OH, THAT'S RIGHT! NOPE, HAVEN'T FOUND OUT A **THING!** YOU SURE YOU HAVE ENOUGH BLANKETS?

YES, MA'M. SIGH. WELL, THANKS ANYWAY, MIZ 'POSSUM! IF THERE'S EVER ANYTHING I CAN **DO** --

AS A MATTER OF **FACT**, I'M ON MY WAY OVER TO MIZ HEDGEHOG'S PLACE, 'N' I WAS WONDERIN' IF YOU'D MIND WATCHIN' TH' KIDS?

ALL **RIGHT!** WE'RE GONNA STAY WITH FONE BONE!

ME?! BUT. . . I DON'T KNOW ANYTHING ABOUT BABY 'POSSUMS!

IT'LL JUST BE FOR AN HOUR OR TWO! YOU BOYS BE **GOOD** NOW!

DON'T WORRY ABOUT **US**, MOM!

WELL . . . C'MON, GUYS. YOU CAN HELP ME PUT THE **FINISHING** TOUCH ON MY HOUSE!

RUN INSIDE WHERE IT'S WARM . . . I'LL JUST BE A SECOND!

WHOOP!

YIPPEE!

THERE WE GO! COZY AS AN IGLOO! BY THE TIME THIS MELTS, IT'LL BE **SPRING**, AN' THEN I'M **OUTTA** HERE!

SMASH! CRASH!

HEY, GUYS! TAKE IT **EASY** IN TH--

CRUNCH

THOSE RAT CREATURES WOULD HAVE TO BE PRETTY STUPID TO FOLLOW ME ON TO THIS FRAIL, LITTLE BRANCH!

STUPID, STUPID RAT CREATURES!!

UH ... WELL ... IT WAS NICE MEETING YOU, BUT I BETTER GO FIND TH' KIDS!

WHOA.

DON'T WORRY ABOUT THE KIDS. THEY'RE SAFE.

GO STRAIGHT DOWN THE HILL. IT'S A SHORTCUT TO MIZ 'POSSUM'S HOUSE.

...UH ...SURE! THANKS!

!

HEY! HOW'D YOU KNOW I WAS LOOKING FOR MIZ 'POSSUM'S KIDS?!

BONE!

BONE! THERE YOU ARE! WE CAME AS FAST AS WE COULD! ARE YOU ALL RIGHT?

YAY!

HE'S SAFE!

I'M OKAY... I HAD A LITTLE RUN-IN WITH A **DRAGON**, BUT THE IMPORTANT THING IS THAT WE'RE ALL SAFE!

A **DRAGON**? REALLY?

GET OUTTA TOWN!

SEE HOW HE IS WITH TH' KIDS? HE'S ALWAYS GOT A STORY!

IT'S NOT ENOUGH THAT HE CHASED OFF THOSE **BULLIES**... NOW HE'S TURNED IT INTO A YARN WITH A **DRAGON** IN IT!

ISN'T THAT PRECIOUS?

WHAT WAS THAT?

OH! I'M SORRY, BONE! TEE HEE! GO AHEAD AN' TELL TH' BOYS ABOUT TH' FEROCIOUS FIRE-BREATHING DRAGON!

YEAH! TELL US! WERE YOU SCARED?

OF **COURSE** I WAS!

HE'S SO MODEST!

AND BRAVE!

WHAT HAPPENED, FONE BONE? DID YOU **KILL** TH' DRAGON?

WHAT HAPPENED TO YOUR HAT? DID THE DRAGON DO IT?

HE'S PULLIN' OUR TAILS! EVERYBODY KNOWS DRAGONS ARE MAKE-BELIEVE!

AREN'T THEY?!

THAT'S ENOUGH QUESTIONS FOR NOW. UNCLE BONE MUST BE **VERY TIRED**. LET'S ALL GO HOME WHERE IT'S WARM AND SAFE, AND THEN BONE CAN TELL US ALL ABOUT HIS **ADVENTURE**!

MAYBE HE'D LIKE TO STOP AND CLEAN UP FIRST.

OH, YES! BY ALL **MEANS!** THERE'S A NICE, HOT **SPRING** JUST BACK OVER TH' HILL! WHY DON'T YOU STOP THERE TO FRESHEN UP! C'MON ALONG, BOYS! SAY THANK YOU TO UNCLE BONE!

THANK YOU!

DID HE REALLY SEE A DRAGON?

NOW, DEAR...

HMMF! DID **TOO** SEE A DRAGON!

WHAT DO THEY **THINK?** I LIT MY **HEAD** ON FIRE TO KEEP WARM?

...AN' HOW COME THAT DRAGON KNEW I WAS BABYSITTING TH' **'POSSUM** KIDS? WHAT'S HE DOIN'? **FOLLOWIN'** ME AROUND?

THIS PLACE IS **TOO** WEIRD! THE FIRST SIGN OF SPRING I SEE... **POW!** I'M TAKIN' OFF **RIGHT** THROUGH THOSE MOUNTAINS! WITH OR **WITHOUT** MY COUSINS!

SNAP!

UH, OH. WHAT WAS THAT?

♪ MMMMMM ♪

FOOM!

OW! OW!

SSSSSSSSSS

WHAT HAPPENED?

DON'T BE AFRAID! I WON'T HURT YOU!

C'MON DOWN! WE'LL SHARE THE POOL!

HELLO.

UM . . . ARE YOU **NEW** AROUND HERE?

FONE BONE! WHAT'S YOURS?!

PLEASED TO MEET YOU, FONE BONE! MY NAME IS THORN.!

THORN. THAT'S **BEAUTIFUL!** THOR--

THORN?! YOU'RE THORN? DO YOU KNOW A LITTLE BUG NAMED **TED?!**

WHY, YES! I KNOW TED! HE'S A **VERY** GOOD FRIEND OF MINE!

HOTCHA! THIS IS GREAT!

I'VE BEEN LOOKIN' FOR YOU ALL **WINTER**!!

YOU HAVE? WHY?

TED! HE TOLD ME TO FIND YOU! HE SAID THAT YOU KNOW **EVERYTHING**!

WELL, THAT CERTAINLY **SOUNDS** LIKE TED.

GREAT! THEN YOU CAN HELP ME AND MY COUSINS GET BACK TO **BONEVILLE**?

COUSINS? YOU MEAN THERE'S **MORE** OF YOU?

YEAH! THEY'RE STUCK IN THIS VALLEY, TOO! BUT I HAVEN'T SEEN EITHER ONE OF 'EM SINCE WE GOT HIT BY THAT SWARM OF **LOCUSTS**!

YOU DON'T SAY.

Y'KNOW... I **SHOULD'VE** ASKED THAT **DRAGON** IF **HE'D** SEEN MY COUSINS!

YOU SHOULD'VE ASKED **WHO**?

THE **DRAGON**! OH . . . WAIT A MINUTE! **I** GET IT! YOU DON'T BELIEVE IN DRAGONS, **DO** YOU?

NO. SHOULD **I**?

NEVER MIND! I DON'T **CARE**!

ONCE I'M BACK IN **BONEVILLE**, I'LL NEVER EVEN HAVE TO **THINK** ABOUT DRAGONS OR THIS CRAZY VALLEY **AGAIN**!

WELL, I'D **LIKE** TO HELP. . .

WELL, C'MON! THERE'S NO TIME TO LOSE!!

. . .BUT. . . I'VE NEVER **HEARD** OF BONEVILLE. THERE **IS** A LITTLE VILLAGE DOWN THE ROAD CALLED BARRELHAVEN . . . DOES THAT HELP?

. . .WHAT'S WRONG?

NOTHIN'

FONE BONE?

OH... I DON'T BELONG IN THIS FOREST. MY HOME'S ON THE OTHER SIDE OF THE MOUNTAINS...

I'M SURE WE CAN GET YOU THROUGH THE MOUNTAINS AS SOON AS THE SNOW MELTS!

IT'S NOT JUST THAT! EVEN IF I **COULD** GET THROUGH THE MOUNTAINS, I'D **NEVER** FIND MY WAY BACK ACROSS THE DESERT. YOU WERE MY LAST HOPE.

WELL, LET'S JUST CONCENTRATE ON FINDING YOUR COUSINS. YOU'RE **SURE** THEY'RE HERE IN THE VALLEY?

PRETTY SURE, UNLESS THE RAT CREATURES GOT 'EM.

DID YOU SAY **RAT CREATURES**?

LET ME GUESS... YOU DON'T **BELIEVE** IN RAT CREATURES.

OH, YES I **DO**! HAVE YOU SEEN ONE **RECENTLY**?

I SAW **TWO** OF 'EM! TH' DRAGON CHASED 'EM OFF!

NOW LISTEN TO ME... THIS IS IMPORTANT! YOU'RE NOT FOOLING AROUND? YOU **REALLY** SAW TWO RAT CREATURES?

YEAH! I REALLY SAW A **DRAGON**, TOO! LOOK AT MY **HEAD**! WHAT DO YOU THINK **THIS** IS? A **TAN**?!

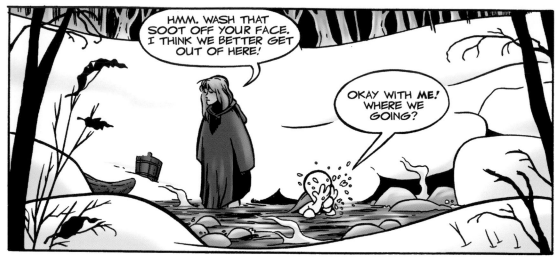

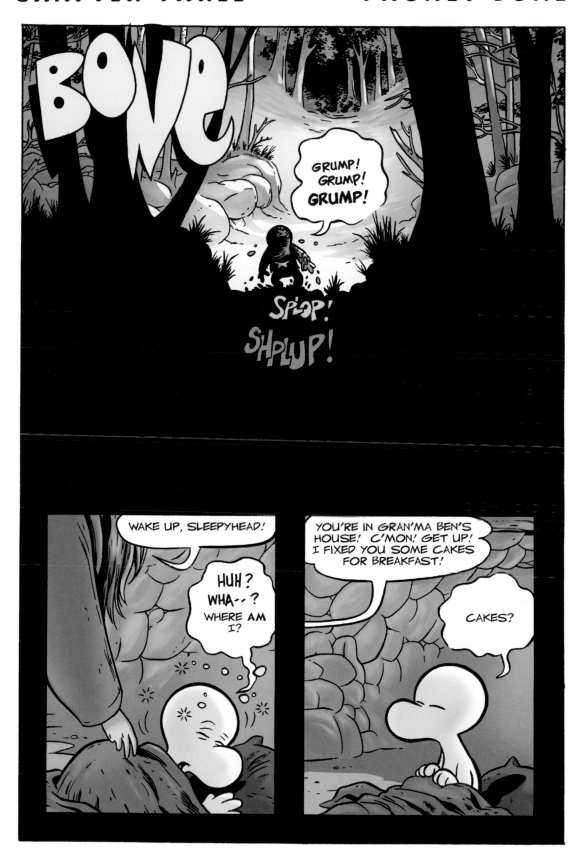

MY! YOU MUST'VE **ENJOYED** YOUR FIRST NIGHT IN A HOUSE AFTER SLEEPING IN THE **WOODS**! YOU DIDN'T EVEN **HEAR** ME WHEN I CAME DOWNSTAIRS!

CAKES?

HERE'S YOUR CAKES! AND HERE'S SOME TEA!

THENK YOU.

HELLO? ARE YOU **AWAKE** YET, FONE BONE? IT'S **ME**, THORN!

THORN?

AH! YOU'RE AWAKE! GOOD! NOW EAT YOUR BREAKFAST! WE'VE GOT A LOT TO **DO** TODAY! GRAN'MA BEN IS COMING HOME FROM THE VILLAGE, AND I WANT TO CLEAN THE PLACE UP BEFORE SHE GETS HERE!

SHE'S COMING HOME **TODAY?**

THAT'S **RIGHT!** SHE GOES INTO **BARRELHAVEN** EVERY SPRING TO SHOW OFF HER BEST **RACING COWS!**

YOUR GRAN'MA RACES **COWS?!**

YEAH! SHE'S PRETTY **GOOD**, TOO! THERE'S HARDLY A COW IN THE WHOLE **VALLEY** THAT CAN BEAT HER IN A **100-YARD DASH!**

HUH! I'M **DEFINITELY** LOOKING FORWARD TO **MEETING** THIS LADY!

OH, IT'S A **BIG EVENT** HERE IN THE SPRING! PEOPLE BET **CHICKENS** AND **GOATS** -- SOME FOLKS BET THEIR WHOLE LIVESTOCK ON HER! IF YOU WANT TO MAKE A GOOD IMPRESSION, BE SURE TO COMPLIMENT HER ON HER **COWS!** SHE'S **REAL** PROUD OF HER COWS!

I'LL TRY TO REMEMBER THAT.

NOW, IF YOU'RE DONE EATING, WHY DON'T WE GO GET SOME WATER?

OKAY BY ME! LET'S **DO IT!**

IF YOU FINISH UP THE DISHES, I'LL GO SPLIT SOME FIREWOOD.

!

NOW **WAIT** A MINUTE, THORN!

WHAT?

WHERE **I** COME FROM, WHAT **YOU** JUST SAID IS **BACKWARDS!**

CHOPPIN' FIREWOOD IS A **MANLY** THING! AN' SINCE **I'M** THE MAN, **I'LL** DO THE **MANLY** THING!

WHAT "MANLY" KIND OF THING DO YOU CALL THAT?

CHIN-UPS! GO DO TH' DISHES!

HOW ABOUT IF WE GET THE FIREWOOD **LATER**?

SIGH.

SO . . . DO YOU THINK YOUR GRAN'MA WILL MIND ME **STAYIN'** WITH YOU GUYS? I MEAN-- I DON'T WANNA CAUSE ANY PROBLEMS!

SHE WON'T MIND! SHE WOULDN'T MAKE YOU GO BACK OUT IN THE **WOODS** -- ESPECIALLY WITH THOSE **RAT CREATURES** AROUND!

I HOPE NOT.

JUST DO ME ONE FAVOR! WHEN GRAN'MA BEN GETS HERE, **TRY** NOT TO MENTION YOUR FRIEND THE **DRAGON**!

WHY NOT?

BECAUSE DRAGONS DON'T **EXIST**, THAT'S WHY!

WHAT DO YOU **MEAN**? YOU BELIEVE IN **RAT CREATURES**! WHY DON'T YOU BELIEVE IN **DRAGONS**?

BECAUSE **EVERYBODY** BELIEVES IN RAT CREATURES! BUT **YOU'RE** THE ONLY ONE WHO'S EVER SEEN A **DRAGON**!

I DON'T BELIEVE IT!

HEY!

COME BACK HERE WITH MY **BUCKET**, YOU!

FONE BONE? WHAT ARE YOU DOING?

I'M COMIN'! I'M COMIN'!

HERE... WHAT DO YOU WANT ME TO DO WITH THIS?

OH! THAT'S MY **KNAPSACK!** I RAN BACK TO MY PLACE LAST NIGHT TO GET MY BOOKS!

YOU HAVE **BOOKS** IN HERE?

YEAH. WHEN ME AN' MY COUSINS GOT RUN OUT OF BONEVILLE, I PACKED SOME STUFF FOR US TO READ...

I **LOVE** BOOKS! OOH! WHAT ARE **THESE?!**

JUST SOME COMIC BOOKS. I BROUGHT THOSE FOR SMILEY BONE.

I'VE NEVER **SEEN** ONE BEFORE!

YOU **HAVEN'T**? YOU MUST'VE HAD A DEPRIVED CHILDHOOD. **THESE** I BROUGHT FOR PHONEY BONE . . . THEY'RE **FINANCIAL MAGAZINES!**

DIDN'T YOU BRING ANYTHING FOR YOURSELF?

SURE! THIS IS **MOBY DICK!** IT'S MY **FAVORITE BOOK!** I'VE READ IT **THREE TIMES!**

WHAT'S IT ABOUT?

UH . . . ARE YOU **SURE** YOU WANT TO KNOW? EVERY TIME I TRY TO TELL PEOPLE ABOUT MOBY DICK THEIR **EYES** GLAZE OVER!

TRY ME.

OKAY! IT'S ABOUT A WHALING VOYAGE, AN' THIS GUY **ISHMAEL** ~~~~

Z

HA. HA. **VERY** FUNNY.

WHAT ELSE HAVE YOU GOT IN HERE?

LET'S SEE . . . A BLANKET . . . AN OLD MAP THAT SMILEY FOUND . . . . . .

THAT'S ABOUT **IT!** THE ONE THING I DIDN'T BRING ENOUGH OF WAS **FOOD** AND **WATER!** WELL, TH' **TWO** THINGS . . . .

WHY ARE YOU MAKING THAT FACE?

I DON'T KNOW . . . . SOMETHING ABOUT THIS MAP IS FAMILIAR . . .

REALLY? SMILEY FOUND IT OUT IN TH' DESERT RIGHT BEFORE WE GOT SPLIT UP.

IT REMINDS ME OF A DREAM I USED TO HAVE . . .

WHOA. AND YOU THINK **MY** STORIES ARE STRANGE!

ARE YOU OKAY?

I'M FINE, LET'S JUST FORGET IT. C'MON, GRAN'MA WILL BE HERE SOON . . .

GRUMP!

SPLOP

SPLOOOSH

OOOH! WAIT'LL I GET MY HANDS ON THAT COUSIN OF MINE!

I CAN'T **BELIEVE** FONE BONE WOULD JUST **LEAVE** ME OUT HERE WANDERING AROUND HELPLESS AND HUNGRY!

I'LL BET HE'S BACK IN BONEVILLE **RIGHT NOW.** SITTING IN **MY** HOUSE, EATING **MY** FOOD!

GLORP!
RUMBLE!
GRRRR

GROWL!

HEY! **SHUT UP**! I JUST ATE A **STICK** AN HOUR AGO! WHAT DO YOU **WANT** FROM ME?!

SLURK GUKK BURRRP!

SIGH.

WHAT A **TRAVESTY!** TH' MOST **CHERISHED** AND **RESPECTED** (NOT TO MENTION WEALTHIEST!) BONE IN BONEVILLE-- OUT IN TH' WOODS-- FENDING OFF TH' ELEMENTS WITH HIS BARE HANDS!

FORCED TO EKE OUT A MISERABLE EXISTENCE AMIDST TH' ROCKS 'N' MUD!!

OH, CRUEL, CRUEL, FATE! WHY HAVE YOU ABANDONED YOUR MOST BELOVED SON ?!

GOD, I PITY ME.

HEY, YOU! WAKE UP!

MM?

THE NAME'S PHONEY BONE ... TH' **RICHEST** BONE IN BONEVILLE! YOU'VE PROBABLY **HEARD** OF ME! I'M LOOKIN' FOR A GUY NAMED FONE BONE. YOU SEEN HIM?

HEY! LET'S KICK THAT PEA-SIZED **DINOSAUR BRAIN** INTO HIGH GEAR, HUH?

WOULD IT HELP IF I ASKED TH' QUESTION AGAIN **SLOWER?**

HAVE......**YOU**.....

...SEEN FONE BONE..... .....A-**ROUND?**

UH, HEY, THERE, MISTER! MAYBE YOU BETTER LET **ME** HELP YOU!

MAYBE I **BETTER!** IT COULD BE **DAYS** BEFORE TH' MESSAGE REACHES **THIS** GUY'S BRAIN!

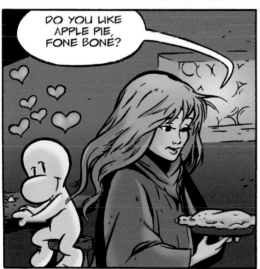

DO YOU LIKE APPLE PIE, FONE BONE?

LIKE IT? IT'S MY FAVORITE **HOBBY!**

WELL, DON'T GET **TOO** EXCITED!

THIS IS FOR GRAN'MA -- SHE **LOVES** MY SPECIAL APPLE PIE...

...AND WE WANT TO BE **REAL** NICE TO GRAN'MA BEFORE WE ASK ABOUT YOU **STAYING HERE!**

CLINK
CLINK

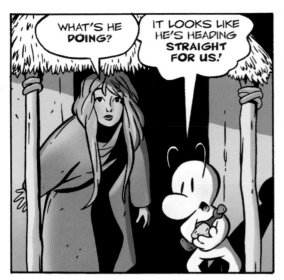

WHAT HAPPENED TO **PHONEY**?

-- UH, OH --

I **THINK** HE'S IN THE **FIREPLACE!**

I'M COMIN', PHONEY!

HURRY, GRAN'MA! HE'S **STUCK** IN THE FIREPLACE!

OH, MY GOODNESS! HE'LL RUIN TH' DINNER!

HANG ON! I'LL GET YOU OUT!

FONE BONE! SAVE ME! THAT CRAZY OLD LADY TRIED TO **KILL ME!!**

WELL, BLESS MY **BUTTONS!** WHAT HAVE WE GOT HERE?

WATCH OUT! DON'T LET HER GET AHOLD OF YOU!

H-- H'LO, MA'M!

DO **YOU** LIKE COWS? I KNOW YOUR **FRIEND** DOESN'T.

I DON'T LIKE TO **RIDE** 'EM, YOU OL' BAT!

FONE BONE **LOVES** COWS!

SORRY, DEAR. YOU CAN'T KEEP HIM.

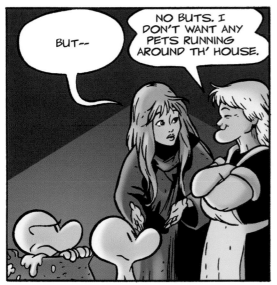

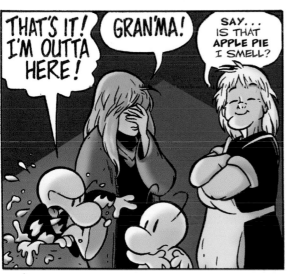

GRAN'MA, THEY'RE **BONES!** THEY COME FROM A PLACE CALLED BONEVILLE! AND THEY NEED OUR HELP TO GET **BACK!**

WHERE'S SMILEY?

SMILEY? I THOUGHT HE WAS WITH **YOU!**

YOU HAVEN'T SEEN HIM SINCE WE SPLIT UP? BUT I **KNOW** HE'S IN TH' VALLEY! I FOUND ONE OF HIS **CIGAR BUTTS!**

TH' LAST TIME I SAW THAT CHOWDERHEAD, HE WAS SAYIN' HOW **COOL** IT WAS THAT WE WERE ABOUT TO BE PULVERIZED BY INSECTS!

YEAH! THAT'S TH' LAST TIME **I** SAW HIM, TOO. . .

AW, QUIT YER **WORRYIN'!** WHY DON'T YA INTRODUCE ME TO YER **GOOD-LOOKIN'** FRIEND, HERE?

OH! UH. . . PHONEY, THIS IS THORN! THORN, PHONEY.

SO, WHAT'VE YOU BEEN DOIN' WITH MY COUSIN? YOU TWO GOT A LITTLE **THING** GOIN', OR WHAT?

PHONEY!

NO, HUH? FIGURES! WHAT'D YA **DO? BORE** HER TO DEATH TALKIN' ABOUT MOBY DICK?

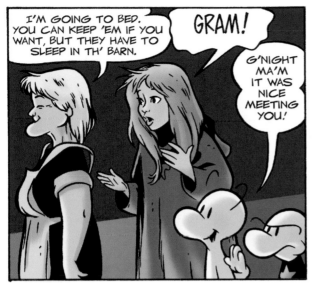

I'M GOING TO BED. YOU CAN KEEP 'EM IF YOU WANT, BUT THEY HAVE TO SLEEP IN TH' BARN.

GRAM!

G'NIGHT MA'M IT WAS NICE MEETING YOU!

FONE BONE, COULD I TALK TO YOU FOR A MOMENT? OUTSIDE?

YES.

WELL, GO AHEAD! I AIN'T STOPPIN' YA!

THIS ISN'T GOING QUITE THE WAY WE **PLANNED**, IS IT? TELL ME. . . IS HE **ALWAYS** LIKE THIS?

PRETTY MUCH.

HMM. GRAN'MA'S GOING BACK TO **BARRELHAVEN** IN A FEW DAYS FOR THE SPRING FESTIVAL. IF WE CAN JUST KEEP THOSE TWO **CALM** UNTIL **THEN**, WE CAN ALL GO INTO TOWN TOGETHER TO LOOK FOR YOUR OTHER COUSIN.

DON'T WORRY! I CAN HANDLE PHONEY!

GO BACK IN THE HOUSE AND KEEP AN **EYE** ON HIM. I HAVE TO GO GET SOME FRESH WATER FOR GRAN'MA TO WASH UP WITH . . .

OKAY, PHONEY! WE HAVE TO GET A COUPLE OF THINGS STRAIGHT---

COME ON! A LITTLE HONEST WORK ISN'T GOING TO KILL YOU!

A **LITTLE**?! THAT CRAZY OL' LADY IS RUNNIN' OUR **BUTTS** OFF! MILK TH' COWS! **FEED** TH' COWS! TAKE CARE OF TH' **CHICKENS**!

GRAN'MA BEN IS **FEEDING** US **AND** LETTIN' US STAY IN HER BARN! TH' **LEAST** WE CAN DO IS HELP OUT!

TH' BARN **STINKS**, AND IT'S **DRAFTY**! IF IT WASN'T FOR TH' **FOOD**, I'D RATHER TAKE MY CHANCES BACK OUT IN TH' **WOODS**!

WE'RE GONNA **END UP** IN TH' WOODS IF YOU DON'T CLEAN THIS UP AN' GET ANOTHER BUCKET OF **MILK**!

I SHOULD'VE **KNOWN** YOU WOULDN'T UNDERSTAND! YOU NEVER HAD ANY **REAL** MONEY! YOU DON'T KNOW WHAT IT'S **LIKE** TO LOSE EVERYTHING! **YOU** DON'T KNOW WHAT IT'S LIKE TO BE **BROKE**!

I'M **HERE**, AREN'T I? BESIDES, YOU'RE NOT **BROKE**! YOU'VE STILL GOT A WAD OF BILLS ON YOU!

ONLY A COUPLE OF THOUSAND. . . STILL, THEY **DO** GIVE ME **SOME** COMFORT! LOOK! AREN'T THEY BEAUTIFUL?

AAAAH!

THEY'RE GETTING **WRINKLED**! I'M TELLIN' YA, FONE BONE, I CAN'T **TAKE** MUCH MORE OF THIS!!

IT'S NOT FOR MUCH **LONGER**! AS SOON AS WE FIND SMILEY BONE WE'RE GONNA GET OUTTA HERE! UNTIL **THEN**, JUST **TRY** NOT TO GET US KICKED OFF TH' FARM, OKAY?

ALL RIGHT, ALL RIGHT. COOL YER JETS! I'LL TRY NOT TO CAUSE ANY TROUBLE.

GOOD! I'VE GOTTA GO FIND **THORN** . . . I PROMISED I'D HELP HER CHURN BUTTER TODAY!

YEAH, YEAH. STICK SOME HAY IN MY TEETH AN' CALL ME GOOBER!

CHEER UP, PHONEY! **BREAKFAST** WILL BE READY SOON!

RRRRR.

MORNIN', BONE!

GOOD MORNIN', GRAN'MA! YOU ALL SET FOR OUR BIG TRIP TO **BARRELHAVEN** TOMORROW?

I'M STILL **PACKIN'**-- I SEEM TO BE MISSING A PAIR OF **BLOOMERS**, THOUGH . . . YOU AN' YOUR COUSIN WOULDN'T KNOW ANYTHING ABOUT THAT, WOULD YOU?

NO, MA'M!

HMMF. HOW ARE THINGS GOIN' IN TH' **BARN** THIS MORNIN'? ANY MORE TROUBLE?

UH... **NO.** PHONEY'S JUST GETTING TH' MILK **NOW**, I THINK!

THAT'S GOOD. WE'VE GOT A TIGHT SCHEDULE ----※

YES, MA'M! THORN AND I ARE GOING TO CHURN BUTTER, AND BAKE THESE LITTLE BREAD THINGS WITH STUFF IN 'EM TO TAKE ON TH' JOURNEY-

OH, NO . . . .

WHAT? DON'T YOU WANT TH' BREAD THINGS?

IT'S NOT TH' **BREAD**, BONE! IT'S TH' **GITCHY FEELIN'**! -- IT JUST COME **AT** ME OUTTA TH' **BLUE!**

TH' **GITCHY FEELIN'**? WHAT'S THAT?

TH' **GITCHY**! IT'S A **TERRIBLE** FEELIN' THAT MAKES YOUR HEAD **SWIM**, AN' YOUR LEGS **WOBBLE**! IT'S A POWERFUL **OMEN** OF BAD **THINGS** TO **COME!**

. . .THERE . . . IT'S STARTIN' TO PASS. MAYBE WHATEVER'S GOIN' TO HAPPEN WON'T BE SO BAD. . .

ARE YOU OKAY?

IT'S GONE NOW. BUT TH' GITCHY FEELIN' IS **NEVER** WRONG! YOU KEEP AN EYE ON THAT COUSIN OF YOURS, YOU HEAR?

YES MA'M!

PHONEY! DID YOU DO SOMETHING WITH GRAN'MA BEN'S **BLOOMERS**?

YEH, I TOOK 'EM OFF TH' CLOTHES-LINE AND NAILED 'EM UP ON TH' SIDE OF TH' BARN.

YOU DID WHAT?!!

I KINDA MADE A LITTLE HOLE IN TH' WALL, AND THOSE WERE THE BIGGEST THINGS I COULD FIND TO COVER IT UP!

YOU'RE REALLY **PUSHIN'** IT, **THIS** TIME, PHONEY!

YOU CAN'T TALK THAT WAY TO ME! I'M YOUR **COUSIN**! I'M TH' **RICHEST BONE** IN **BONEVILLE**!

YOU **WERE** TH' RICHEST BONE IN BONEVILLE! AN' IT WAS YOUR **MONEY-GRUBBIN' SCHEMES** THAT GOT US **INTO** THIS MESS, REMEMBER?

DO YOU **HAVE** TO KEEP BRINGING THAT UP?! SO I GOT US RUN OUT OF BONEVILLE, AND A **LYNCH MOB** CHASED US FOR TWO WEEKS! **JEEZ!** ONE LITTLE MISTAKE, AND I GOTTA HEAR ABOUT IT TH' REST OF MY **LIFE**?!

MAYBE YOU'LL THINK **TWICE** NEXT TIME BEFORE YOU BUILD AN **ORPHANAGE** ON A **HAZARDOUS WASTE LANDFILL**!!

WHAT IS **WRONG** WITH **THAT**?! THAT'S **TWO** COMMUNITY SERVICES **ROLLED INTO ONE**!! IT WAS TH' **ULTIMATE TAX SHELTER**!

YOU **NEVER** LEARN, DO YOU?

I **SHOULDA** STUCK WITH MY FIRST IDEA!

WHAT? COMBINING A **SLAUGHTERHOUSE** WITH A **PETTING ZOO**?! OH, YEAH! **THAT** WAS BRILLIANT!

AHH! WHAT DO **YOU** KNOW?

CAN'T YOU MAKE IT THROUGH **ONE MORE DAY** WITHOUT GETTING US IN **TROUBLE**? WE'RE GOIN' INTO TOWN WITH GRAN'MA **TOMORROW!**

WHAT ARE WE WAITIN' FOR HER FOR? LET'S BLOW THIS POPSICLE STAND **NOW!**

TOMORROW IS TH' FIRST DAY OF TH' **SPRING FAIR!** THIS'LL BE OUR **BEST SHOT** AT FINDING SMILEY BONE!

GRAN'MA SAID THAT **LAST** WEEK PEOPLE WERE ALREADY COMIN' IN FROM **ALL OVER** TH' VALLEY- - - SETTIN' UP **BOOTHS** AN' GETTIN' **READY!**

WELL, I FIGURE -- IF SMILEY'S SOMEWHERE IN TH' VALLEY, HE'S **BOUND** TO HAVE HEARD ABOUT GRAN'MA'S **COW RACE!** YOU **KNOW** HOW MUCH HE LIKES TO BET ON **RACES!**

HO -- BACK UP! YOU MEAN PEOPLE ACTUALLY BET **MONEY** ON THAT OL' BAG TO BEAT A **COW** IN A **FOOTRACE?**

I **KNOW!** IT'S **CRAZY,** BUT THORN SAYS IT'S A BIG **DEAL** HERE! SOME FOLKS BET EVERYTHING THEY'VE **GOT!**

OKAY, FONE BONE! **I'LL** BE GOOD! I POSITIVELY **GUARANTEE** YOU WON'T HEAR ANOTHER **PEEP** OUTTA ME ALL DAY!

YEP, YOU WON'T HEAR A **PEEP** OUTTA **ME**, 'CAUSE **I** AIN'T GONNA **BE** HERE!

FONE BONE WON'T MIND IF I BORROW A FEW OF HIS THINGS . . . I MIGHT NEED 'EM ON MY WAY TO TOWN . . .

SOUNDS LIKE A LOTTA **MONEY'S** GONNA CHANGE HANDS TOMORROW, AN' I DON'T SEE WHY GRAN'MA BEN SHOULD **HOG** IT ALL!

NO, SIRREE! IF THERE'S **BOOKMAKIN'** TO BE DONE, **I'M** TH' MAN TO **DO** IT!

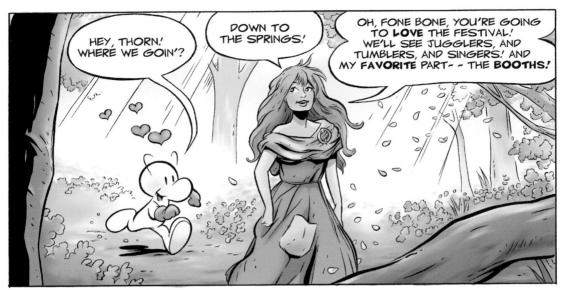

RRRR. THERE WAS A **PATH** HERE A **SECOND** AGO! WHAT HAPPENED TO IT?

CRACK

CRUNCH

SNAP

WHY DOESN'T SOMEBODY BUILD SOME **ROADS** IN THIS PLACE?!

HMM. MAYBE I SHOULD LOOK INTO THAT. . . .

I COULD BUILD A **TOLL ROAD!**

YEAH! I CAN ALMOST **HEAR** THOSE LITTLE COINS CALLING OUT TO ME **NOW** - -

HELLO, BONÉ!

OVER HERE! IN TH' TREE!

WHAT ARE YOU KIDS DOIN' HANGIN' AROUND HERE? GET A JOB!

SORRY, MISTER! WE THOUGHT YOU WERE SOMEONE ELSE!

WE THOUGHT YOU WERE FONE BONE!

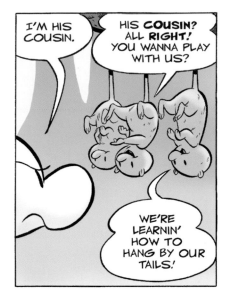

I'M HIS COUSIN.

HIS **COUSIN?** ALL **RIGHT!** YOU WANNA PLAY WITH US?

WE'RE LEARNIN' HOW TO HANG BY OUR TAILS!

NO, THANKS. I'M ON MY WAY INTO TOWN.

HEY, MISTER! YOU KNOW TH' **WAY** INTO TOWN?

YEAH. WHY?

IT'S **THAT** WAY.

OH! RIGHT!

THANKS, KID! WHEN I COME BACK, I'LL BRING YOU A **CARROT!**

A CARROT? WHAT'S HE THINK WE ARE? RABBITS?

WHAT A DORK.

LUCKY THING I RAN INTO THOSE KIDS! AS SOON AS I'M BACK ON TH' RIGHT PATH, I SHOULD GET TO BARRELHAVEN IN **NO TIME!**

TH' FIRST THING I GOTTA DO IS HIT TH' LOCAL TAVERN, AN' FIND OUT WHO'S IN TOWN TO BET ON TH' RACE . . .

SNIFF

SNIFF! SNIFF! OOOH! MAN! SOMETHING AROUND HERE SURE **STINKS!**

JEEZ! IT'S GETTIN' **WORSE!**

WHOA.

WHAT TH' **HECK** ARE **THOSE** THINGS?

UH, OH! SOMEBODY'S COMIN'!

GET UP, YOU TWO.

ZZRT SNORT! WHA--?

GET UP BEFORE I CRUSH YOUR HEADS.

KINGDOK!

KINGDOK?

SIRE! WHAT ARE **YOU** DOING HERE? MAY I KISS YOUR FEET? I WISH I HAD SOME **QUICHE** I COULD OFFER YOU--

W-WOULD YOU LIKE SOME OF THE SMALL DEAD THING I FOUND UNDER A BUSH? I WAS SAVING HALF FOR LATER, BUT YOU'RE MORE THAN WELCOME--

QUIET! I'VE HAD SCOUTS OUT LOOKING FOR YOU TWO!

Y-YOU HAVE? HOW FLATTERING! **I'M** FLATTERED! ARE YOU FLATTERED?

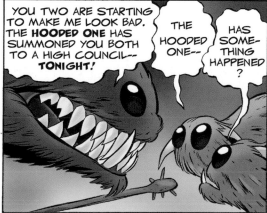

YOU TWO ARE STARTING TO MAKE ME LOOK BAD. THE **HOODED ONE** HAS SUMMONED YOU BOTH TO A HIGH COUNCIL-- **TONIGHT!**

THE HOODED ONE--

HAS SOMETHING HAPPENED?

HE HAS RECEIVED WORD THAT THE ONE WE SEEK-- THE SMALL, BALD CREATURE WITH THE **STAR** ON ITS CHEST-- HAS BEEN SEEN IN THE VALLEY!

HE **HAS?!** BUT-- BUT--

HE WAS LAST SEEN IN **YOUR** TERRITORY!

COME WITH ME!

YES, SIRE! RIGHT AWAY!

EVERYTHING'S READY FOR TOMORROW. I JUST WISH I COULD SHAKE THIS **GITCHY FEELIN'** I GOT!

DID YOU FIND TH' LITTLE SQUIRT?

NO. AN' MY **BOOTS** AN' **KNAPSACK** ARE MISSING, TOO.' I THINK HE WENT INTO TOWN WITHOUT US!

WE LOOKED FOR HIM, BUT THERE'S NO SIGN OF HIM ON THE ROAD. WE WENT ALL THE WAY TO OLD MAN'S CAVE BEFORE IT GOT TOO DARK. I'M SURE WE'LL FIND HIM AT THE FAIR TOMORROW.

HMM. I DON'T LIKE IT. AN' THERE'S A BAD MOON OUT TONIGHT, TOO.

RUN BACK TO TH' BARN, AN' GET YOUR BLANKET. I THINK YOU BETTER COME IN TH' HOUSE WITH US TONIGHT.

OKAY.

....APPROACH ME....

....I HAVE RECEIVED WORD THAT THE ONE WE SEEK HAS BEEN SEEN IN YOUR TERRITORY....
...HOW IS IT THAT YOU HAVE NOT BROUGHT HIM TO ME?

WE -- WE HAVE NOT SEEN THE ONE WHO BEARS THE STAR --

BUT ON SEVERAL OCCASIONS WE HAVE SEEN ONE WHO IS MUCH LIKE HIM IN DESCRIPTION.... HE IS CALLED FONE BONE....

WE FIRST SAW HIM ON THE WESTERN RIDGE -- ON THE DRAGONS' STAIR-- WE HAVE SEEN THIS NEW CREATURE TWICE MORE IN THE VALLEY NEAR THE WATERFALL....

DID YOU THINK THIS WAS INSIGNIFICANT? WHY DID YOU NOT CAPTURE THE CREATURE AND BRING IT TO THE COUNCIL?

...HE BEARS NO STAR...

WE TRIED TO CAPTURE HIM, MASTER.....BUT HE IS CHARMED! HE IS UNDER THE PROTECTION OF THE GREAT RED DRAGON!

WE TRIED TO SPY.... BUT THE DRAGON TREADS A WIDE CIRCLE AROUND HIM...

THE CREATURE IS ON A SMALL FARM NEAR THE HOT SPRINGS... HE STAYS WITH THE OLD COW WOMAN ...MOTHER BEN.....

...., THESE ARE GRAVE TIDINGS....IT WOULD NOT BE WELL FOR THE DRAGON TO LEARN OF OUR PLANS....

....IF WE MUST RISK A CONFRONTATION..... WE MUST DO IT NOW... WHILE THE DRAGON'S SUSPICIONS SLEEP....

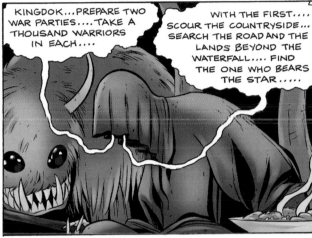

KINGDOK...PREPARE TWO WAR PARTIES....TAKE A THOUSAND WARRIORS IN EACH....

WITH THE FIRST.... SCOUR THE COUNTRYSIDE... SEARCH THE ROAD AND THE LANDS BEYOND THE WATERFALL.... FIND THE ONE WHO BEARS THE STAR.....

....IF THE DRAGON IS STILL WATCHING....THIS ACTIVITY WILL DRAW HIM OFF...LEAVING THE OLD COW WOMAN UNGUARDED.....

SEND THE SECOND PARTY TO THE FARMHOUSE .... DESTROY IT....... ...KILL THE NEW CREATURE...

LET US HOPE THAT THE DEATH OF THIS FONE BONE WILL CAUSE THE DRAGON TO LEAVE THE VALLEY AND RETURN TO DEREN GARD....

...GO NOW.... WE ATTACK TONIGHT!

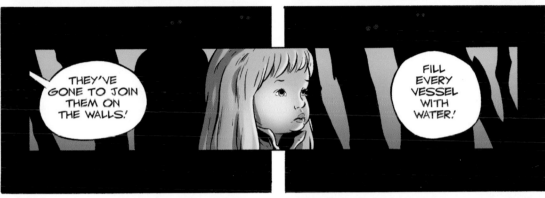

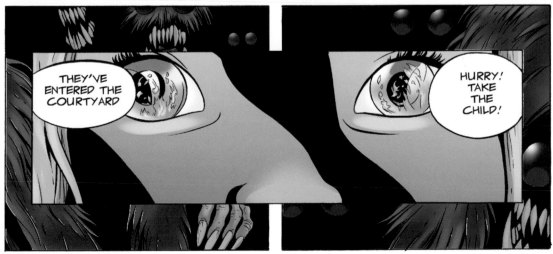

HOW MANY ARE THERE?

DON'T KNOW . . . HERE, BONE. HOLD THIS!

OH, MAN!

I CAN HEAR 'EM MOVIN' **AROUND** OUT THERE!

THORN, DEAR . . . BRING ME A POKER FROM THE FIREPLACE — AND YOU BETTER PUT SOME **SHOES** ON . . .

DO YOU HAVE A **PLAN**, GRAN'MA?

I HAVE AN IDEA THAT MIGHT WORK.

OKAY, CHILDREN! LISTEN CLOSELY! THIS IS WHAT WE'RE GOING TO DO . . .

— WHEN I SAY RUN . . . . . . YOU **RUN!** GOT THAT?

WHAT?!

THAT'S YOUR **PLAN?** RUN **WHERE?**

READY?

HERE WE GO!

CRASSSH SPLINTER

K-K-RR-K

OKAY, KIDS! RUN!

CRUNCH

UH...

NOW, BONE!

WE CAN'T JUST **LEAVE** YOU HERE!

COME **ON**, FONE BONE!

DON'T WORRY ABOUT **ME**--!

BIF!

SPLAT!

I FOUGHT TH' RATS BACK IN TH' **BIG** WAR!

OHMYGOSH

THUD THUD! WAK!

OHMYGOSH

OHMYGOSH

GET UP! GET UP!

CREEEAK

IT **IS** YOU! THANK **GOODNESS** I'VE **FOUND** YOU!!

YA **MEAN** IT, PHONEY? YOU'RE **HAPPY** TO SEE ME?

DARN RIGHT!! FONE BONE WOULDN'T LET ME **LEAVE** THIS STUPID VALLEY UNLESS I **FOUND** YOU FIRST!

AW, SHUCKS -- IT'S GOOD TO SEE YOU, **TOO**, CUZ!

THIS CALLS FOR A **TOAST!** LET ME BUY YOU A **DRINK**, OL' **BUDDY!**

OKAY BY ME, OL' **PAL!**

HERE'S TO GOIN' **HOME!**

TO BONEVILLE!

CLINK

TO BONEVILLE!

GLUG! GLUG!

AHH!

WHADDYA SAY WE HAVE ANOTHER ROUND ON **YOU**, OL' FRIEND!

SMEK

SMEK

SURE! WHY **NOT?** I GOT A FEELIN' MY **LUCK'S** ABOUT TO **CHANGE!** -- **GUESS** WHERE FONE BONE IS **RIGHT NOW!** HE'S WITH **GRAN'MA BEN!** YOU KNOW -- TH' OLD LADY THAT RACES **COWS!**

AH! YOU'RE IN TOWN FOR TH' **COW RACE!** ME TOO! THERE'S GONNA BE SOME HEAVY **BETTIN'** GOIN' ON!

SO I'VE HEARD!

IS ANYBODY DOIN' TH' **BOOKMAKIN'**?

NOT YET... BUT FROM WHAT I'VE PICKED UP-- YOUR FRIEND **GRAN'MA** IS TH' **ODDS-ON** FAVORITE!

GREAT! PERFECT! HOW MUCH TIME DO WE HAVE?

ONE WEEK.

EXCELLENT! I GOT AN **IDEA** THAT'LL MAKE US A **LOTTA** MONEY!

UH, OH! I HOPE THIS ISN'T GONNA BE ONE OF THOSE **SILLY** IDEAS YOU USED TO PULL BACK IN **BONEVILLE!**

WHAT?! WHAT ARE YOU **TALKIN'** ABOUT? **WHAT** SILLY IDEAS?!

REMEMBER TH' **FIRST** TIME YOU GOT US RUN OUT OF TOWN? YOU OPENED UP A CHAIN OF FRANCHISES -- **BONE ENVIRONMENTAL:** NUCLEAR REACTOR AND ENDLESS SALAD BARS!

THAT WASN'T A **SILLY** IDEA! TH' **LETTUCE** WOULDN'T SPOIL FOR **DECADES!**

WELL, IT WAS **PRETTY** SILLY!

OH, YEAH, YOU'RE A **BRILLIANT** JUDGE!

NOW-- WHERE ARE WE GONNA FIND A **COW SUIT?**

WHAT? I GET TO WEAR A **COW SUIT?! COOL!** HAVE ANOTHER **BEER**, PARTNER!

WHAT'S THIS?

TWO **EGGS**, PAL! WHAT? DID TH' PRICE GO UP?

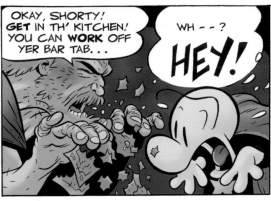

OKAY, SHORTY! **GET** IN TH' KITCHEN! YOU CAN **WORK** OFF YER BAR TAB...

WH -- ?

HEY!

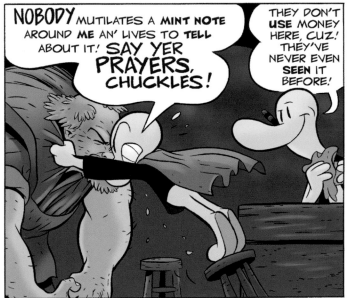

NOBODY MUTILATES A **MINT NOTE** AROUND **ME** AN' LIVES TO **TELL** ABOUT IT! **SAY YER PRAYERS, CHUCKLES!**

THEY DON'T **USE** MONEY HERE, CUZ! THEY'VE NEVER EVEN **SEEN** IT BEFORE!

COME AGAIN?

THEY TRADE **GOODS** AND **SERVICES**. IT'S A **BARTER SYSTEM!**

CHUCKLES WANTS **REAL EGGS!**

YOUR BUTT IS **MINE**, BALDY!

SMILEY -- **WHY** DID YOU KEEP GIVING ME BEER? YOU **KNOW** I DON'T CARRY **DAIRY PRODUCTS !!**

UH, OH! LOOKS LIKE I MISSED SOME OF THOSE DIRTY GLASSES!

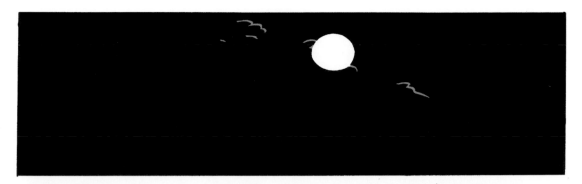

THEY'RE CIRCLING US!

WHAT DO YOU WANT?!

WE WANT THE SMALL CREATURE.....

YOU CAN'T HAVE HIM!

GO AWAY!

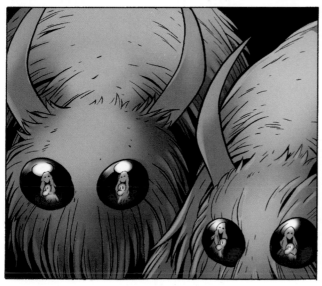

GIVE IT TO US...

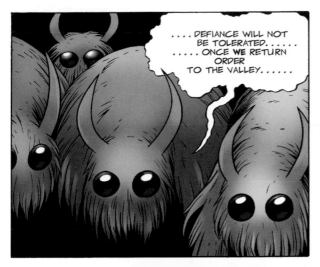

.... DEFIANCE WILL NOT BE TOLERATED...... ...... ONCE **WE** RETURN ORDER TO THE VALLEY......

STAY BACK!

SNIFF! SNIFF!

WAIT A MINUTE! WAIT A MINUTE!

DO YOU **SMELL** THAT?!

IT'S BRIMSTONE! IT'S THE **DRAGON!** HE'S **HERE!**

OH, NO.

RELAX, THORN! EVERYTHING'S GONNA BE **OKAY!**

FONE BONE! WHAT ARE YOU DOING?!

I KNOW **YOU** DON'T BELIEVE IN DRAGONS, BUT **THESE GUYS** DO! WATCH **THIS!**

OKAY, FELLAS! PARTY'S **OVER**! BREAK IT UP! **LET'S GO**! TH' DRAGON'LL BE HERE **ANY MINUTE** NOW, AN' YOU DON'T WANNA **BE HERE** WHEN HE SHOWS UP!

JUST THE **SIGHT** OF TH' DRAGON SENDS THESE GUYS INTO A **PANIC**! THEY RUN LIKE THEIR **FUR'S** ON FIRE!

ARE YOU STILL **HERE**? **GO ON!** **SHOO**!

I SMELL NOTHING...

WHAT ARE YOU **TALKIN'** ABOUT? YOU DON'T SMELL BRIMSTONE?

SSSSSS

NO.

SNIFF! SNIFF! **THAT'S WEIRD!** I DON'T SMELL IT ANYMORE, EITHER!

LOOK OUT!

AARR

OOF!

CHUNK

WHY, LOOK, TED. IT'S A MEETING OF THE NEW COMMUNITY LEADERS.

OOH! A TOWN MEETING! DOES WE GITS TA VOTE? I JES LOVES TA VOTE!

HISSS! STAY BACK, WORM!

OUR NUMBERS ARE TOO GREAT!

EVEN FOR YOU!

FUNNY YOU SHOULD MENTION THAT-- HOW MANY WARRIORS DO YOU HAVE BETWEEN HERE AND THE WATERFALL? A THOUSAND? TWO THOUSAND?

HIYA, BONES! HEY, THORNY! C'MON OVER HERE!

SSSSSS

I BELIEVE THIS VIOLATES OUR AGREEMENT...

YOU WOULD NOT BE SO BOLD IF KINGDOK WERE HERE!

YOU RUN AND TELL KINGDOK THAT I'M WATCHIN' HIM!

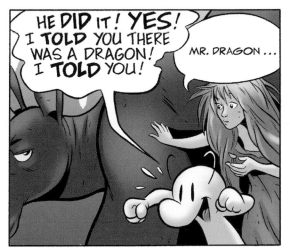

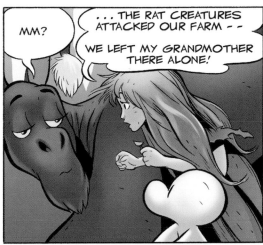

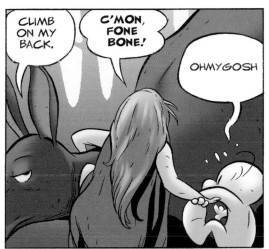

A **REAL** DRAGON, GRAN'MA! LOOK!

I CAN SEE.

HELLO, DRAGON.

HELLO, ROSE. IT'S BEEN A WHILE.

YEP.

WELL . . . LOOKS LIKE EVERYTHING'S UNDER CONTROL HERE. GUESS I'LL BE GOIN'.

YEP.

C'MON, TED.

GRAN'MA! WHAT ARE YOU **DOING**?! THE DRAGON JUST SAVED OUR **LIVES!**

NOT NOW, THORN. MR. BONE FROM BONEVILLE AN' I HAVE TO HAVE A LITTLE **CHAT!**

AND **YOU** HAVE A LOT OF THINGS TO DO BEFORE WE LEAVE FOR TH' **SPRING FAIR!**

THE **FAIR**?! YOU'RE NOT STILL WORRIED ABOUT YOUR **COW RACE**?!

WHAT ABOUT **PHONEY BONE** AN' **SMILEY**? WE HAVE TO **FIND** THEM!

BONE AND I WILL HITCH UP TH' CART. **YOU** BE A SWEETHEART AND PUT OUT TH' **FIRE** ON TH' ROOF!

SHE'S NOT EVEN **LISTENING** TO US! CAN YOU **BELIEVE** SHE WANTS TO GO TO TH' **FAIR**?!

ARE YOU **KIDDING**? I STILL CAN'T GET OVER TH' **FACT** THAT SHE HAS A **FIRST NAME!**

DEAR ... I'M NOT A **COMPLETE** NINCOMPOOP! WE'LL BE **SAFER** IN TOWN! **AND**, WITH ANY LUCK, WE'LL BE ABLE TO FIND HIS **COUSINS!**

BUT --

PLEASE, THORN! WE **HAVE** TO GO! WE DON'T KNOW IF THEY'RE **SAFE!**

YOU'RE RIGHT! I'LL TAKE CARE OF THE ROOF!

WE PACKED EVERYTHING LAST NIGHT, SO TH' LUGGAGE IS ALREADY OUT IN TH' BARN. COME JOIN US WHEN YOU GET DONE.

C'MON, BONE!

GRAN'MA? WHAT **WAS** THAT WITH YOU AN' TH' DRAGON? DO YOU GUYS **KNOW** EACH OTHER?

I'LL ASK TH' QUESTIONS! I WANNA KNOW WHY THOSE MONSTERS WERE AFTER **YOU** ... AN' I WANT TH' **TRUTH!**

I HAVE **NO** IDEA! **HONEST!** I'VE NEVER DONE **ANYTHING** TO THEM!

WHAT ABOUT THAT SHIFTY **COUSIN** OF YOURS? YOU THINK **PHONEY BONE** MIGHT'VE HAD SOME DEALIN'S WITH 'EM?

NO, MA'M! WE DON'T **HAVE** RAT CREATURES BACK WHERE WE COME FROM!

IN FACT, WE NEVER EVEN **HEARD** OF RAT CREATURES BEFORE WE GOT RUN OUT OF BONEVILLE!

WELL, ACTUALLY, **I** WASN'T RUN OUTTA BONEVILLE -- **PHONEY** WAS! SMILEY AN' I JUST HELPED HIM GET AWAY!

WHAT'D HE **DO**?

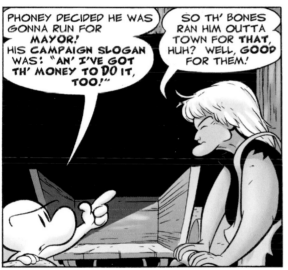

PHONEY DECIDED HE WAS GONNA RUN FOR **MAYOR**! HIS CAMPAIGN SLOGAN WAS: "AN' I'VE GOT TH' MONEY TO **DO** IT, TOO!"

SO TH' BONES RAN HIM OUTTA TOWN FOR **THAT**, HUH? WELL, **GOOD** FOR THEM!

NO.

ANYBODY CAN RUN FOR MAYOR. EVEN **PHONEY**!

THAT GREEDY, LITTLE **LOUDMOUTH**? NOT IN MY TOWN HE COULDN'T!

WELL, HE CAN IN BONEVILLE. **ANYWAY**, HE WANTED TO MAKE THE **OFFICIAL** ANNOUNCEMENT A BIG **SOCIAL EVENT**, SO HE DECIDED TO THROW A PICNIC DOWN ON TH' BANKS OF TH' **ROLLING BONE** RIVER ...

THERE'S A **BEAUTIFUL** PARK THERE WITH GREEN, SLOPING LAWNS THAT STRETCH TO THE EDGE OF TH' WATER. IT'S JUST FAR ENOUGH AWAY FROM TH' **HUSTLE** AN' **BUSTLE** OF DOWNTOWN BONEVILLE THAT THERE WOULDN'T BE ANY **DISTRACTIONS**!

PHONEY INVITED **EVERYBODY** IN TOWN -- AN' HE PROMISED **FREE FOOD** FOR ANYONE WHO SHOWED UP! PRETTY SOON, TH' **PICNIC** WAS TH' **TALK** OF BONEVILLE!

THEN TH' BIG DAY ARRIVED, AN' TH' **WHOLE TOWN** TURNED OUT! TH' KIDS WERE PLAYIN' UNDER TH' TREES, AN' THE WOMEN WORE SUNBONNETS AN' FANCY DRESSES! THE PICNIC WAS OFF TO A **PERFECT START!**

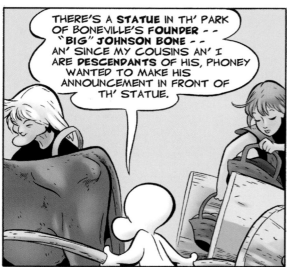

THERE'S A **STATUE** IN TH' PARK OF BONEVILLE'S **FOUNDER** -- "BIG" JOHNSON BONE -- AN' SINCE MY COUSINS AN' I ARE **DESCENDANTS** OF HIS, PHONEY WANTED TO MAKE HIS ANNOUNCEMENT IN FRONT OF TH' STATUE.

... AND JUST TO **ADD** TO TH' FESTIVITIES, PHONEY HAD A **50**ft. **BALLOON** MADE OF HIMSELF! TH' BALLOON WAS TIED TO OL' "BIG" JOHNSON!

FASTEN THAT END THERE, WOULD YOU, BONE?

EVERYTHING WAS GOIN' **GREAT!** FOLKS WERE LISTENIN' TO TH' **FIREHOUSE** BAND AN' ENJOYIN' TH' SUNSHINE! TH' FOOD WAS PASSED OUT AN' THERE WERE PLENTY OF **PRUNE TARTS** FOR **EVERYONE!**

PRUNE TARTS?

YEAH. YOU KNOW PHONEY. HE GOT A GOOD DEAL ON SOME PRUNES FROM A DISCOUNT **PRUNE BROKER!**

OF COURSE!

SO ANYWAY, HE MAKES THE **ANNOUNCEMENT**, RIGHT? HE GETS UP AND DECLARES HIS CANDIDACY FOR **MAYOR** OF **BONEVILLE!**

I STILL THINK **THAT'S** WHEN THEY SHOULD'VE RUN HIM **OUT!**

THAT'S WHEN A GUST OF WIND CAME OFF TH' RIVER AND PULLED TH' **BALLOON** LOOSE! THE STATUE CAME OFF ITS **BASE** AN' WAS DANGLIN' OFF TH' BALLOON'S **ANKLE!** ALL OF A **SUDDEN**, THIS GIANT, INFLATABLE PHONEY BONE STARTED MOVING TOWARD THE **CROWD!**

OH, MY!

YEAH, IT WAS **AMAZING!** MY FIRST-GRADE TEACHER, **MISS CRAB-BONE**, WAS THE FIRST TO **PANIC!** SHE STARTED SCREAMING AND RUNNING BACK AN' FORTH! THE BALLOON CHASED HER INTO TH' **RIVER** BEFORE SMILEY AND I COULD LET THE **AIR** OUT OF IT!

...IT WAS **AWFUL!** EVERYONE WAS **STUNNED!** AT FIRST NOBODY MOVED! THEY JUST **SAT** THERE WITH THIS LOOK OF **HORROR** ON THEIR FACES!

AN' **THAT'S** WHEN THEY RAN YOU OUTTA TOWN.

NO. THAT'S WHEN TH' **BAD PRUNES** KICKED IN...

... I JUST WANT YOU TO **KNOW** ... I'VE BEEN **WORKING** ON THE **PLAN**! I BEEN SPREADIN' **RUMORS** ALL DAY THAT GRAN'MA BEN IS **TOO OLD** TO WIN TH' RACE THIS YEAR!

IS ANYBODY **BUYIN'** IT?

I'M TH' **BARTENDER**! THEY **GOTTA** BELIEVE ME!

THIS IS **TOO EASY!** WE'LL COVER ALL TH' **BETS**, AND THEN WHEN GRAN'MA **WINS**, WE'LL BE **RICH!**

OF COURSE, WHEN GRAN'MA GETS INTO **TOWN**, EVERYBODY'S GONNA **SEE** SHE'S **PERFECTLY FIT!**

I'VE GOT THAT COVERED WITH PHASE **TWO** :

THE MYSTERY COW!

A **COW** THAT WE'LL **BUILD UP** IN EVERYBODY'S IMAGINATION THAT **CAN'T BE BEAT!**

WAIT! IS **THAT** TH' PART WHERE I GET TO WEAR TH' **COW SUIT** ?! OH, **JOY!**

YEAH, **THAT'S** TH' PART! BUT YOU'RE GONNA **THROW** TH' **RACE**! REMEMBER! WE **WANT** GRAN'MA BEN TO **WIN!**

WELL, **NATURALLY**, I'M LOOKING FORWARD TO WEARIN' A **COW SUIT** -- BUT WHAT DO **YOU** GET OUT OF IT? AFTER **ALL**, THE LOCALS DON'T USE **MONEY**! THEY TRADE GOODS 'N' SERVICES!

IT **DOES** SOUR MY PLANS FOR AMASSING A **HUGE** FORTUNE AND RETURNING TO BONEVILLE IN **TRIUMPH** ... **STILL**, THE PLAY IS TH' THING!

IF ALL THESE YOKELS **HAVE** ARE **POULTRY PRODUCTS**, THEN I'LL **TAKE IT !!**

BESIDES, I HAVE A **HANKERIN'** TO TAKE TH' PROPRIETOR OF THIS FINE ESTABLISHMENT TO TH' **CLEANERS!** YOU **WITH** ME?

SURE! IT DOESN'T MAKE ANY DIFFERENCE TO ME! BUT THEN ... NOT MUCH **DOES!**

GOOD. NOW GET BACK OUT THERE AND KEEP SPREADIN' **RUMORS!**

AN' QUIT BRINGIN' ME DIRTY DISHES TO WASH!

PHONCIBLE P. BONE.....AT **LAST** I HAVE FOUND YOU.....

WHO, **ME?** HOW DO YOU KNOW MY NAME?

...YOU SHOULD BE GRATEFUL INDEED THAT YOUR FRIENDS INTERFERED ON YOUR BEHALF LAST NIGHT.... I AM FORCED TO USE MUCH MORE SUBTLE METHODS OF CONTACTING YOU....

WHAT TH' **HECK** ARE YOU **TALKIN'** ABOUT?

.... YOUR COUSIN FONE BONE HAS AWAKENED THE GREAT RED DRAGON..... ... FOR THIS ... ... I WILL **KILL** HIM .....

...SO THERE HE IS, OKAY? **ISHMAEL'S** LAYIN' IN HIS BUNK WAITIN' FOR HIS MYSTERIOUS NEW ROOMMATE TO SHOW UP... **SUDDENLY** -- AT LIKE, **3 O' CLOCK** IN TH' MORNING -- TH' DOOR SWINGS **OPEN**... AN' **THERE**, STANDIN' IN TH' DOORWAY, WITH TH' LIGHT FROM TH' HALL BEHIND HIM, IS **QUEEQUEG!** AN' HE'S CARRYIN' SHRUNKEN HEADS!!

WHAT'S GOING ON, BACK THERE?

OH... H'LO, THORN.

ARE YOU TALKING ABOUT **MOBY DICK** **AGAIN**?

IT JUST SO HAPPENS THAT GRAN'MA **LIKES** TO HEAR ABOUT **GOOD BOOKS!** SHE **APPRECIATES** FINE LITERATURE!

HEY, GRAN'MA! WAKE UP!

ZZ-SNORT!

WHA -- ARE WE THERE ALREADY?

DOO-OOP!

NOT QUITE. BUT I THOUGHT I SHOULD WAKE YOU UP.

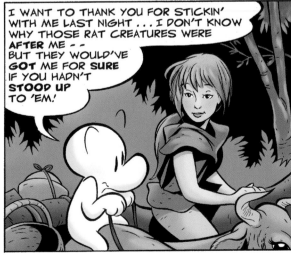

WELL, WELL . . . IT'S ABOUT **TIME!**

HELLO, LUCIUS!

HOW YA DOIN', ROSIE? WAS TH' **ROAD** SAFE? I WAS **WORRIED** ABOUT YA!

TH' ROAD WAS CLEAR . . . EXCEPT FOR YOUR **ROADBLOCK!**

OH! I GOT SOMETHIN' FOR YA! **HERE!** I BEEN SAVIN' IT IN MY POCKET ALL DAY!

OH, AREN'T YOU SWEET!

. . . WELLL . . . . . I HAD A LITTLE EXTRA **TIME** ON MY HANDS THIS MORNING . . .

. . . I GOT A COUPLE OF **DEADBEATS** INSIDE TAKIN' CARE OF TH' **CUSTOMERS** - - IN FACT, THEY LOOK A **LOT** LIKE THIS LITTLE FELLA YOU GOT HERE.

THEY **DO?!**

This book is for Dan Root

YOU KNOW WHAT **I** WANT? SOME **HONEY**! LET'S GO FIND A **HONEY-BOOTH**!

OKAY, THORN.

I DIDN'T KNOW YOU LIKED HONEY SO MUCH!

I **LOVE** IT! AT THE FAIR YOU CAN GET HONEY FROM THE SOUTHERN END OF THE VALLEY -- IT'S **SWEETER** . . .

. . . AND THE **BOYS** WHO **SELL** IT ARE **CUTER**!

YOU KNOW, I'LL BET TH' FOREST IS **FULL** OF HONEY!

C'MON! LET'S GO LOOK FOR A **BEEHIVE**!

THE BEES AROUND HERE ARE TOO BIG! BESIDES! WHAT FUN WOULD **THAT** BE?

SIGH.

OOOH! THERE'S A BOOTH THAT SELLS **DYES**! WE'LL HAVE TO COME BACK HERE LATER!

I BET **I** COULD GET YOU SOME HONEY FOR FREE!

I'M SURE YOU COULD. OH, **LOOK**! THERE'S A **HONEY-SELLER**!

THAT'S ENOUGH! YOU CAN'T TALK TO MY FRIEND THAT WAY!

COME ON, FONE BONE!

WHAT WERE YOU THINKING? I'VE NEVER SEEN YOU ACT THAT WAY BEFORE!

HE STARTED IT WITH THAT CRACK ABOUT MY NOSE!

I DON'T CARE WHO STARTED IT! IT WAS EMBARRASSING!

BUT --

WHEN YOU CAN WALK AROUND THE FAIR WITHOUT GETTING INTO A FIGHT -- COME FIND ME! UNTIL THEN, I'D RATHER BE BY MYSELF!

HONEY!

THIS IS **GREAT!** I'LL GET THORN SOME HONEY **MYSELF!**

HOW HARD CAN IT BE? I JUST NEED SOME **GREEN GRASS** THAT'LL **SMOKE** REAL GOOD WHEN I LIGHT IT . . .

. . . THEN I'LL **WAVE** TH' SMOKE IN FRONT OF TH' HIVE UNTIL TH' BEES FALL **ASLEEP!**

THIS IS GONNA BE LIKE TAKING **CANDY** FROM A **BABY!**

NOW TO JUST **SHIMMY** UP TH' TREE!

YEAH! THEY WERE **GONNA** BET ON GRAN'MA BEN TO WIN TH' RACE, BUT WHEN I TOLD 'EM THE RUMOR YOU **TOLD** ME TO TELL 'EM - - THAT GRAN'MA WAS TOO OLD 'N' DECREPIT TO **WIN** THIS YEAR - - THEY WANTED TO CHANGE THEIR **BETS!**

HOW MUCH? HOW MUCH?

ONE GUY WANTS TO BET A **DOZEN EGGS**, AN' TH' OTHER WANTS TO BET A **PIG!** HAM AN' EGGS, BUDDY! **RIGHT THERE!**

THAT'S **IT!** WE'RE IN **BUSINESS!**

COOL! SO WHAT DO YOU WANT ME TO DO **NOW?**

I'M GONNA NEED A PLACE TO HOLD TH' **GOODS!** UNTIL **THEN**, START TAKIN' THEIR **MARKERS!** THERE'S NO TIME TO LOSE!

HERE . . . GIMME YOUR PAD. I'LL POST SOME **ODDS!**

"MYSTERY COW . . . . . FOUR TO ONE GRAN'MA BEN . . . . . . SIXTY TO ONE"

ALL TH' **OTHER** COWS IN TH' RACE WILL BE SOMEWHERE IN BETWEEN. WHAT DO YOU THINK OF THAT?

I THINK YOU JUST MADE THAT UP.

OF **COURSE** I JUST MADE THAT UP, YOU **MORON!** WE'RE FIXIN' TH' RACE, REMEMBER?!

IT DOESN'T **MATTER** WHAT TH' ODDS ARE, AS LONG AS **NO ONE** BETS ON GRAN'MA BEN.'

-- AND THEN WHEN TH' OL' BAT **WINS**, WE GET TO **KEEP** EVERYTHING.'

WE'LL BE **RICH.'**

RIGHT.' AN' WE'LL SPLIT IT **NINETY/TEN**, JUST LIKE ALWAYS.'

I LIKE TH' CUT OF YOUR **JIB**, MISTER.'

I KNOW YOU DO. NOW GET OUT THERE AN' DRUM UP SOME **BUSINESS**, PARTNER.'

OH, HEY . . . SMILEY.' WAIT A MINUTE.'

THERE WAS SOMETHIN' I WANTED TO ASK YOU ABOUT . . .

ASK AWAY, PARTNER.'

I WAS, UM -- WELL, . . . I WAS JUST **WONDERING** . . . SINCE YOU'VE BEEN IN TH' VALLEY -- HAVE YOU EVER RUN ACROSS ANY BIG, **SMELLY MONSTERS?** WITH POINTY EARS, AN' **GLOWING EYES?** OR A GUY WITH A **HOOD** PULLED DOWN OVER HIS FACE, CARRYIN' A **SCYTHE?**

MONSTERS-- MONSTERS--

BIG, SHAGGY **MONSTERS** WITH **HUGE TEETH** . . . THEY MIGHT'VE BEEN ASKIN' **QUESTIONS** ABOUT ME . . .

HMMM.

JEEZ, SMILEY! YOU HAVE TO **THINK** ABOUT IT? DID YOU SEE ANY MONSTERS OR **NOT?!**

WELL, **SOMETIMES I** SEE STRANGE STUFF, BUT DISTINGUISHING **REALITY** FROM **FANTASY** ISN'T ALWAYS MY STRONGEST SUIT.

FORGET IT, OKAY? GO BACK TO WORK!

HEY, SMILEY!! GET THIS **BLUE PLATE** OUT TO TABLE THREE! MY CUSTOMERS ARE **HUNGRY!**

YES, SIR, MR. DOWN!

I DON'T KNOW WHAT YOU **TWO** ARE **UP** TO, BALDY, BUT I'M KEEPIN' MY **EYE** ON YOU.

YEAH, YEAH.

BY THE WAY . . . I LIKE TH' HAT. IT'S A GOOD LOOK FOR YOU.

RRRRR.

WELL, HOWDY, GRAN'MA BEN! OUT **TRAININ'**, I SEE.

GOTTA KEEP IN **SHAPE**, ED! WHO'S THIS? LOOKS LIKE YOU BROUGHT A NEW **GIRL** WITH YOU!

THIS IS **SUSAN**! I'M GONNA RUN HER AGAINST YOU IN TH' **RACE** THIS YEAR!

AH! MY COMPETITION! HI THERE, SWEETHEART!

WELL, HELLO, MARYLOU! HI, HELEN!

ROSE BEN! AS I LIVE AN' BREATHE! WE WERE JUST TALKING ABOUT YOU!

WE WERE JUST SAYING THAT WE WEREN'T GOING TO BET ON YOU THIS YEAR!

HELLO THERE, JON OAKS! GOOD TO SEE YOU AGAIN!

HI, GRAN'MA! IT'S GOOD TO SEE **YOU** AGAIN, TOO!

SAY, JON, WOULD YOU MIND TELLING ME WHO YOU'RE **BETTIN'** ON IN TH' BIG RACE?

I WAS GONNA BET ON **YOU**, GRAN'MA . . .

BUT NOW I'M SCOUTIN' AROUND FOR A **YOUNGER** CONTESTANT! GOTTA GO WITH A SAFE BET, DON'TCHA KNOW!

SEE YA LATER, GRAN'MA!

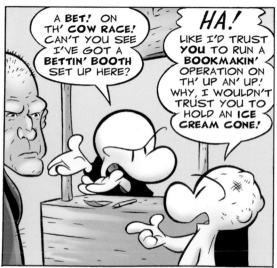

WHY IS SMILEY WEARING A COW SUIT?

I'M NOT SMILEY! I'M A **REAL** COW!

MY WORLD IS CRUMBLING AROUND ME.

MOO!

THINK I'LL CHEW ME SOME **CUD!**

WHAT'S GOIN' ON HERE, PHONEY?

IT'S JUST, UH... PART OF A **PROMOTION** WE'RE DOIN' FOR TH' RACE! **THAT'S ALL!**

I **KNEW** IT! YOU'RE UP TO SOMETHIN', AN' YOU'RE GONNA GET US **RUN OUT** OF TH' VALLEY-- **JUST** LIKE YOU GOT US **RUN OUT OF BONEVILLE!**

OH, **HERE** WE GO AGAIN ABOUT **BONEVILLE!** OKAY, SO A FEW OF MY BUSINESS DEALS WERE A LITTLE **SHAKY** -- IS IT MY FAULT TH' WHOLE TOWN WENT **NUTS** JUST BECAUSE I THREW A **PICNIC** AN' ANNOUNCED I WAS RUNNIN' FOR MAYOR?

THEY WENT **NUTS** BECAUSE THEY **KNEW** TH' ONLY REASON YOU WANTED TO BE **MAYOR** WAS SO YOU COULD PULL OFF EVEN **BIGGER SHAKY BUSINESS DEALS!**

AND BECAUSE YOU SERVED **BAD PRUNES** AT TH' PICNIC AND GAVE TH' WHOLE TOWN TH' **FAST-TRACK SALLIES!**

OKAY, PHONEY, IT'S TIME TO COME CLEAN!

WHAT **ELSE** HAVE YOU DONE?

WHAT DO YOU **MEAN** WHAT ELSE?

YOU KNOW WHAT I MEAN! EVER SINCE WE **GOT** TO THIS VALLEY, GIANT, **RAT-LIKE** CREATURES HAVE BEEN **AFTER** US! I WANNA KNOW WHAT **YOU KNOW** ABOUT IT!

I'M **TELLIN'** YA, FONE BONE, I DON'T KNOW **ANYTHING** ABOUT IT! I KNOW THE RAT CREATURES HAVE BEEN **ASKIN'** ABOUT ME, BUT I DON'T KNOW **WHY!** HONEST!

YEAH? WHAT'S **THAT** SLAVE DRIVER WANT?

HE SAID TO TELL YOU YOUR LUNCH BREAK IS **OVER** . . .

. . . AN' IF YOU'RE NOT BACK BEFORE HE RUNS OUT OF **CLEAN DISHES**, HE'S GONNA TWIST YOUR HEAD OFF YOUR BODY!

WHOOPS!

SORRY, FONE BONE, BUT THIS CONVERSATION IS GONNA HAFTA WAIT!

SMILEY! GET OUT OF THAT **STUPID COW SUIT**, AND TAKE OVER TH' **BETTING BOOTH!**

ALL RIGHT, PHONEY. YOU CAN **KEEP** YOUR LITTLE SECRET FOR NOW . . .

PHOO! WHICH SECRET?

. . . BUT WHEN WE GET BACK TO **BONEVILLE** YOU'RE GONNA COME **CLEAN**, YOU **HEAR ME?**

YEAH, YEAH! SEE YA TONIGHT!

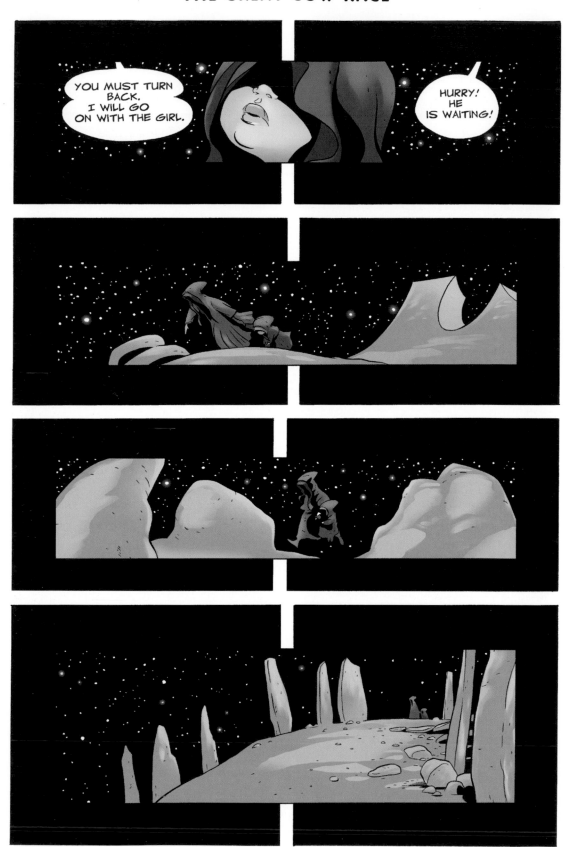

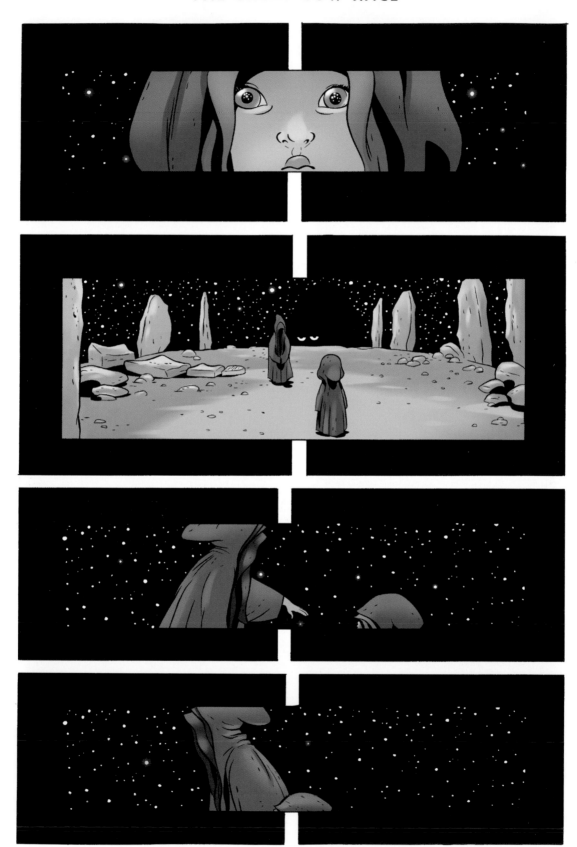

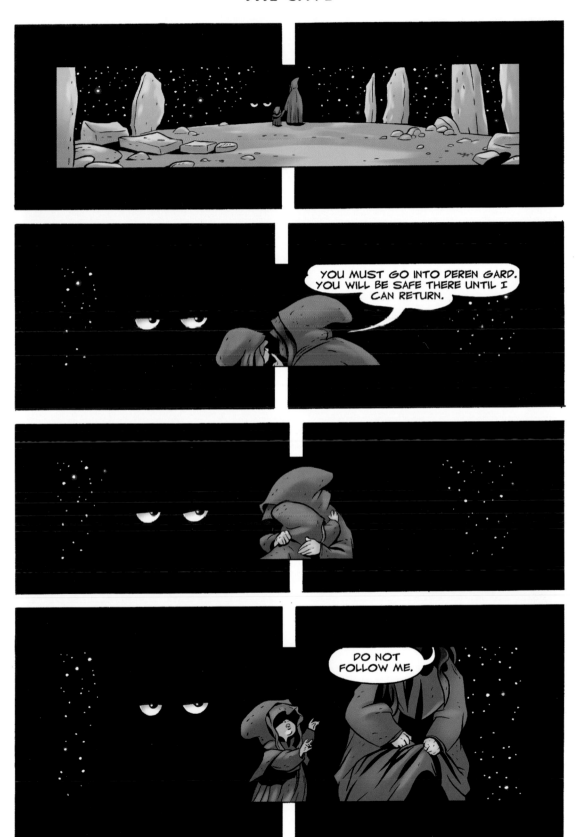

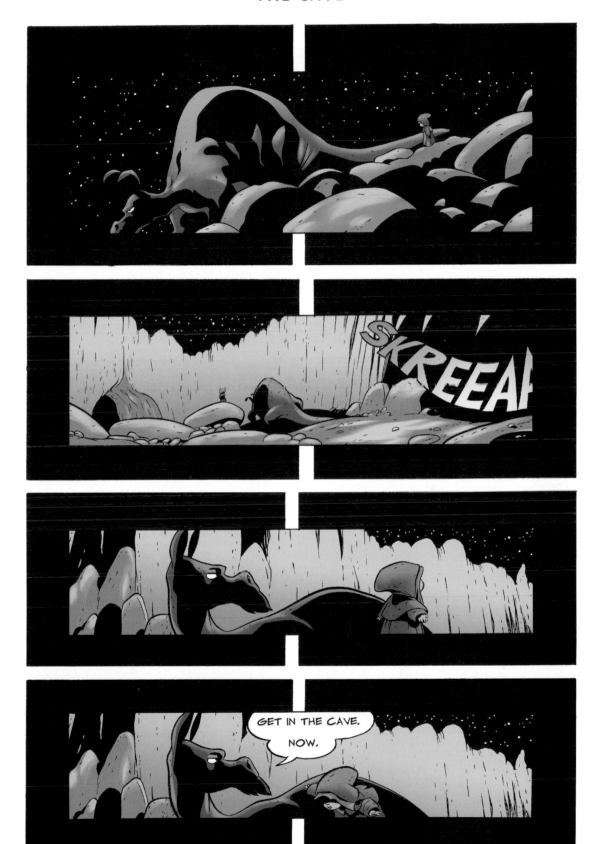

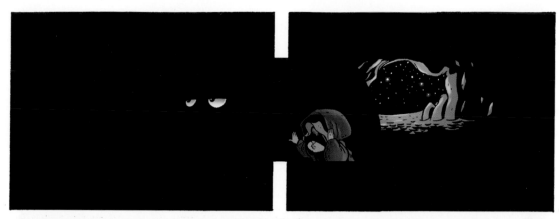

FONE BONE?

ARE YOU AWAKE?

NO.

FONE BONE . . .

MM?

WHAT?

KEEP YOUR VOICE DOWN.

WHAT IS IT, THORN? YOU HAVE ANOTHER WEIRD DREAM?

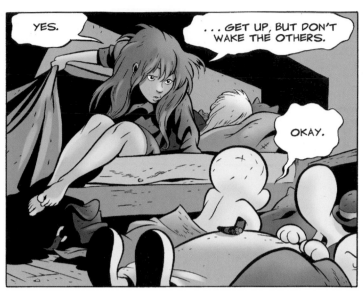

YES.

. . . GET UP, BUT DON'T WAKE THE OTHERS.

OKAY.

DO YOU STILL HAVE THAT OLD MAP THAT YOU AND YOUR COUSINS FOUND OUT IN THE DESERT?

I THINK SO. IN MY KNAPSACK.

HERE IT IS. YOU KNOW . . . WHEN I WAS **LOST** OUT IN TH' DESERT, I ACTUALLY **FOLLOWED** THIS MAP INTO TH' VALLEY!

LET'S SIT AT THE TABLE.

WHEN I WAS A LITTLE GIRL, I USED TO HAVE THIS **ONE** DREAM **OVER** AND **OVER** AGAIN. IN THE DREAM I WAS STANDING IN A **MAGNIFICENT CAVERN** -- SURROUNDED BY **DRAGONS!**

AND NOW YOU'RE STARTING TO HAVE THIS DREAM AGAIN?

YES. AND WHENEVER I **HAVE** IT, IT WAKES ME UP IN THE MIDDLE OF THE NIGHT.

HAVE YOU TOLD GRAN'MA BEN ABOUT THE DREAMS?

YAWN!

I DID WHEN I WAS LITTLE. SHE USED TO TELL ME NOT TO BE AFRAID BECAUSE DRAGONS DON'T REALLY EXIST!

HMM. THAT'S STRANGE. GRAN'MA KNOWS ABOUT DRAGONS!

RIGHT, BUT I DIDN'T KNOW THAT THEN. AND YOU SAW THE WAY SHE AND THE GREAT RED DRAGON WERE ACTING THE OTHER DAY! THOSE TWO KNOW SOMETHING THAT WE DON'T!

YOU THINK IT HAS SOMETHING TO DO WITH THIS MAP?

ALL I KNOW IS I STOPPED HAVING THAT DREAM YEARS AGO -- UNTIL YOU SHOWED UP AND PULLED THAT MAP OUT OF YOUR KNAPSACK!

EVER SINCE THEN THE DREAMS HAVE BEEN BACK -- AND THEY'RE MORE VIVID AND REAL THAN EVER BEFORE!

I STILL DON'T UNDERSTAND WHY SEEING THIS OL' MAP WOULD TRIGGER TH' DREAMS.

I THINK I DO ...

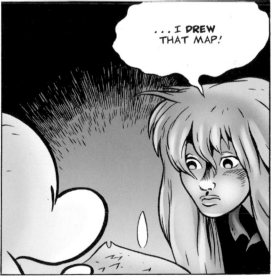

... I DREW THAT MAP!

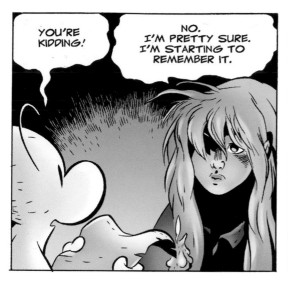

YOU'RE KIDDING!

NO. I'M PRETTY SURE. I'M STARTING TO REMEMBER IT.

I DREW THAT MAP WHEN I WAS IN THE CAVE WITH THE DRAGONS.

WHOA.

WAIT A MINUTE. WHAT ARE YOU SAYING? YOU REALLY **WERE** IN A CAVERN WITH A BUNCH OF DRAGONS? I THOUGHT IT WAS A **DREAM!**

OH, I DON'T KNOW, FONE BONE!

IT'S SO CONFUSING!

OKAY, OKAY. WE'LL GO SLOW WITH THIS . . . SO -- **WHY** DID YOU DRAW THE MAP?

THE DRAGONS WERE HOLDING ME IN THE CAVERN. I DREW THE MAP BECAUSE I HOPED SOMEONE WOULD FIND IT AND COME RESCUE ME.

WHAT DO YOU **MEAN** HOLDING? WERE YOU A **PRISONER?**

I DON'T REMEMBER ANYMORE . . . BUT AT THE TIME I WANTED TO ESCAPE.

HOW **DID** YOU ESCAPE?

ESCAPE? OH, THIS IS **RIDICULOUS,** FONE BONE! I WAS NEVER IN A **DRAGON'S CAVE!** IT WAS JUST A **DREAM!**

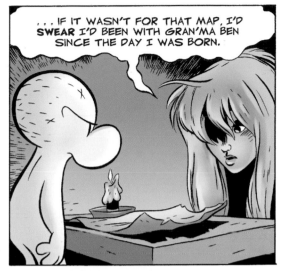

...IF IT WASN'T FOR THAT MAP, I'D **SWEAR** I'D BEEN WITH GRAN'MA BEN SINCE THE DAY I WAS BORN.

WELL, **THERE'S** TH' MAP! I SAY WE WAKE GRAN'MA UP AND **SHOW** IT TO HER!

NO. LET'S WAIT UNTIL AFTER THE RACE. SHE'S GOT ENOUGH TO WORRY ABOUT RIGHT NOW.

LET'S KEEP THE MAP A SECRET FOR NOW ...JUST BETWEEN YOU AND ME, OKAY?

OKAY. IF THAT'S WHAT YOU WANT.

GOOD. LET'S GO BACK TO BED.

- 191 -

GIMME A CUP OF TEA, LUCIUS.

COMIN' RIGHT UP, ROSIE!

ARE YOU OKAY? YOU LOOK KINDA DOWN.

IT'S NOTHING, SWEETY. I'M FINE.

I DON'T THINK SO -- YOU'RE USUALLY **CHOMPIN' AT TH' BIT** THIS CLOSE TO TH' **COW RACE!**

LOOK AT YOU! YOU'RE ALL **SLUMPED** OVER! **C'MON**, ROSIE, YOU DON'T WANT FOLKS TO SEE YOU LIKE THIS!

WHAT **DIFFERENCE** DOES IT MAKE?

YOU WANT PEOPLE TO BET ON **YA**, DON'TCHA? WELL, THEY **WON'T** UNLESS YOU LOOK LIKE A **WINNER!** NOW **SIT UP!**

I APPRECIATE WHAT YOU'RE DOING, DEAR. BUT IT'S TOO LATE. **NOBODY'S** BETTIN' ON ME **ANYWAY!**

OH, THEY'RE **NOT**, ARE THEY? WHO TOLD YOU **THAT?**

EVERYBODY! YOU **MUST'VE** HEARD TALK IN TH' BAR.

YEAH, WELL, I DON'T LISTEN . . .

. . . AN' NEITHER SHOULD YOU! YOU CAN'T LET 'EM GET YOU **DOWN,** ROSIE! TH' ONLY WAY YOU CAN **WIN** TH' RACE IS IF YOU BELIEVE IN **YOURSELF!**

HE'S **RIGHT,** GRAN'MA! DON'T LISTEN TO TH' **RABBLE!** THINK **POSITIVE!**

SINCE WHEN ARE **YOU** ONE OF MY **BOOSTERS,** PHONEY BONE?

I'M A **FRIEND,** GRAN'MA! AN' I **CARE!**

PAY NO ATTENTION TO WHAT THESE FARMERS ARE SAYING! YOU CAN **WIN!** I HAVE **FAITH** IN YOU!

WHAT ARE YOU UP TO, YOU LITTLE **RUNT?**

NOTHING! CAN'T A **FRIEND** WISH A **FRIEND LUCK?**

BOY! THAT WAS **DELICIOUS!** LUCIUS'S MENU CERTAINLY HAS **IMPROVED** SINCE HE HIRED YOUR COUSINS TO WORK IN THE **KITCHEN!**

YEAH, PHONEY ALWAYS WAS A GOOD COOK . . .

SAY, UM . . . THORN? YOU WANNA WALK AROUND TH' **FAIR** TOGETHER TODAY?

OH. GEE, FONE BONE. I'M SORRY. I ALREADY PROMISED **TOM** I'D WALK AROUND WITH **HIM.** YOU REMEMBER TOM - - HE'S THE BOY AT THE **HONEY-SELLER'S** BOOTH.

OH, YEAH. I REMEMBER HIM.

WELL . . . I GUESS I BETTER GET GOING. SEE YOU AT THE COW RACE, OKAY?

OKAY. SEE YA.

HEY! WHAT'S THIS I HEAR ABOUT NOBODY BETTIN' ON ROSE? WHAT'S TH' **MATTER** WITH YOU GUYS? YOU TRYIN' TO HURT HER **FEELINGS?!**

NAW! WE AIN'T TRYIN' TO HURT HER FEELIN'S. BUT **YOU** HEARD TH' RUMORS. GRAN'MA BEN IS **WASHED UP!**

WE KNOW YOU'RE SWEET ON HER, LUCIUS, BUT **NOBODY'S** GONNA BET ON ROSE WHEN TH' ODDS ARE A **HUNDRED TO ONE** AGAINST HER!

A HUNDRED TO ONE?! SEZ WHO?!

ASK YER COOK! HE'S GOT A **BETTIN' BOOTH** SET UP ON TH' FAIRGROUNDS!

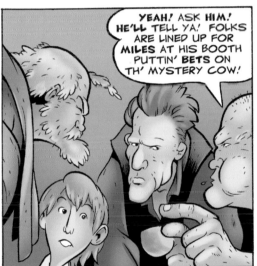

YEAH! ASK HIM! HE'LL TELL YA! FOLKS ARE LINED UP FOR **MILES** AT HIS BOOTH PUTTIN' **BETS** ON TH' MYSTERY COW!

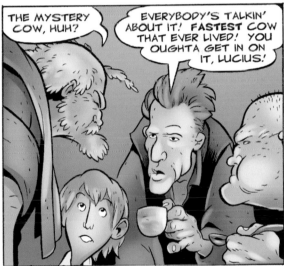

THE MYSTERY COW, HUH?

EVERYBODY'S TALKIN' ABOUT IT! **FASTEST COW** THAT EVER LIVED! YOU OUGHTA GET IN ON IT, LUCIUS!

ANYBODY ACTUALLY **SEEN** THIS MYSTERY COW?

WHAT DO YOU MEAN?

I MEAN HAVE ANY OF YOU JOKERS LAID YOUR OWN **EYEBALLS** ON THIS COW YOU BET YOUR **LIFE'S SAVINGS** ON?

YEAH! **SURE!** WELL . . . **I** HAVEN'T SEEN IT - - BUT **SOMEBODY** MUST HAVE!

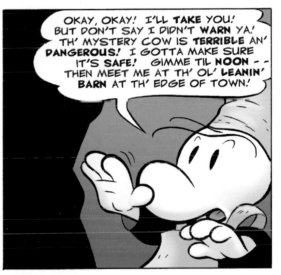

AH! **THERE** HE IS!

TOM! OH, TOM!

THERE YOU ARE, TOM! I WAS LOOKING ALL **OVER** FOR YOU!

OH!

THIS IS **JASMINE!** I'M SHOWIN' HER AROUND TH' FAIR TODAY.

HI.

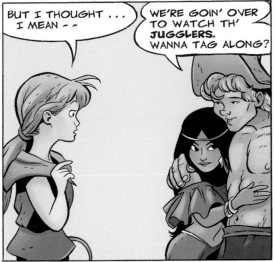

BUT I THOUGHT . . . I MEAN - -

WE'RE GOIN' OVER TO WATCH TH' **JUGGLERS.** WANNA TAG ALONG?

OH - - NO THANKS. I WAS - - UH - - I WAS SUPPOSED TO WALK AROUND WITH MY FRIEND FONE BONE ANYWAY.

OH, YEAH! TH' LITTLE GUY WITH TH' **NOSE!** OKAY, THORN, CATCH YA LATER!

'BYE.

JEEZ!

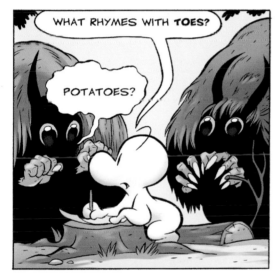

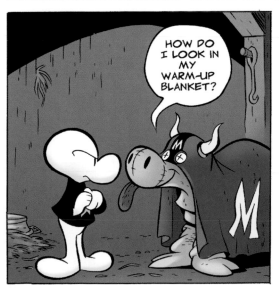

GOOD LUCK, GRAN'MA!
YOU CAN DO IT!
I KNOW YOU CAN!

LUCIUS! HAVE YOU SEEN FONE BONE?

NOT SINCE THIS MORNIN'.

LAST TIME I SAW **HIM**, HE WAS SITTIN' BY HIMSELF AT TH' BREAKFAST TABLE.

FONE BONE WOULDN'T MISS THE COW RACE!

I WONDER WHAT HAPPENED TO HIM?

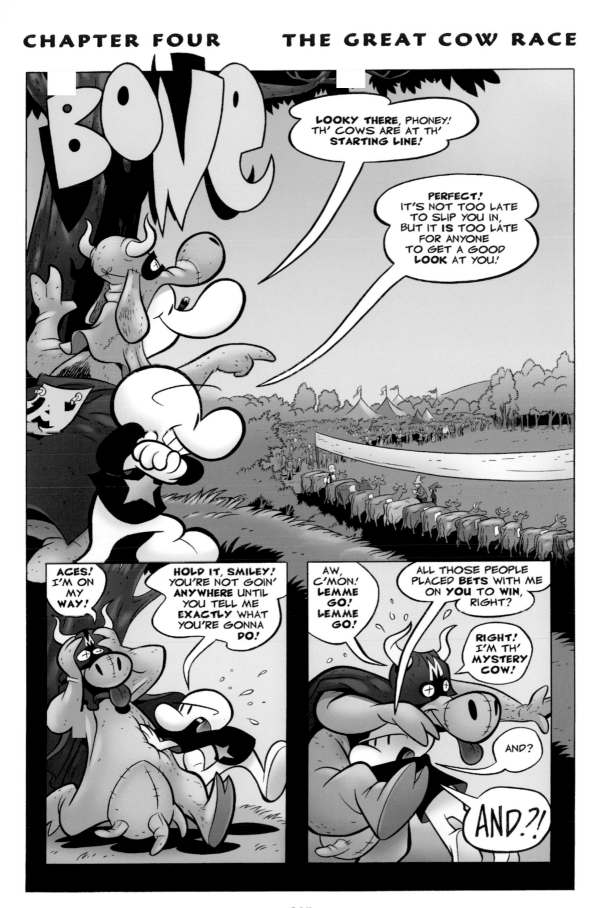

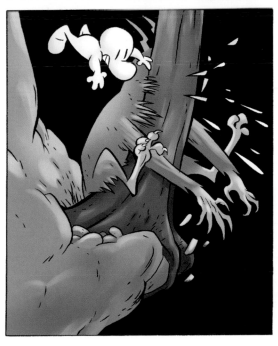

RUN, KIDS! THE RAT CREATURES ARE AFTER ME!

EEEEEE

AAAHRRRR

WHAT'RE WE GONNA DO?!

WE ALL RAN AN' HID LIKE **BABIES**!

WE GOTTA HELP HIM!

WE COULD CUT AHEAD OF 'EM AN' MEET 'EM AT TH' FORK IN TH' ROAD...

THEN WE COULD HANG BY OUR TAILS AN' PULL BONE UP INTO TH' **SMALLER BRANCHES** WHERE TH' RAT CREATURES CAN'T GO!

GOOD IDEA!

SOMEBODY SHOULD TELL MOM!

OKAY! YOU GO FOR HELP!

C'MON'! LET'S GO!

GO! GO! GET THEM!!

H'LO, FONE! I DIDN'T KNOW **YOU** WERE IN TH' RACE!

SHUT UP, SMILEY!

WOULD SOMEBODY PLEASE JUST **KILL** ME?

HERE THEY COME! **WOW!** WHAT **HAPPENED?!**

BEATS ME! YOU GRAB BONE, AN' **I'LL** GRAB HIS COUSIN!

UH, OH --

UH, OH, WHAT?

UH, OH **THAT!**

UH, OH!

CLIP
CLOP
CLIP
CLOP

THE VILLAGERS WON'T FOLLOW US **THIS FAR** AFTER **DARK.**! I THINK IT'S SAFE TO BRING **PHONEY BONE** DOWN NOW.

I'LL GET HIM.

HE'S BEEN AWFUL **QUIET.** YOU THINK HE'S ALL RIGHT?

I **THINK** SO. IT LOOKS LIKE SOME OF THE **EGG** IS HARDENING AND HE CAN'T MOVE HIS **MOUTH.**!

I SAY WE LEAVE HIM THAT WAY.

GET HIM DOWN, THORN!

JUST A MOMENT... THERE!

IT'S ABOUT TIME!! GET ME DOWN FROM HERE!! THIS IS AN OUTRAGE! MY HANDS ARE GOIN' TO SLEEP!

I TOLD YOU TO LEAVE HIM!

PHONCIBLE P. BONE! YOU SHOULD BE GRATEFUL WE GOT YOU AWAY FROM THAT ANGRY MOB AT ALL! WHY, IF GRAN'MA HADN'T PROMISED TO COVER YOUR DEBTS FROM THE COW RACE, THINGS MIGHT'VE BEEN A LOT WORSE THAN BEING TIED TO A STAKE AND HIT WITH EGGS!

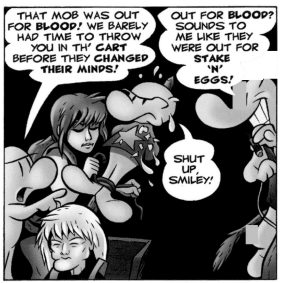

THAT MOB WAS OUT FOR BLOOD! WE BARELY HAD TIME TO THROW YOU IN TH' CART BEFORE THEY CHANGED THEIR MINDS!

OUT FOR BLOOD? SOUNDS TO ME LIKE THEY WERE OUT FOR STAKE 'N' EGGS!

SHUT UP, SMILEY!

HOW COME THEY DIDN'T TIE SMILEY TO A STAKE? HE WAS TH' ONE IN TH' COW SUIT!

AN' A STRIKING FIGURE OF A COW I MADE AT THAT!

YER BOTH IN TROUBLE!

AN' TO WORK OFF YER DEBTS, YOU AN' SMILEY ARE GONNA SPLIT YER TIME BETWEEN FARM CHORES AT GRAN'MA'S, AND WASHIN' DISHES FOR ME AT TH' TAVERN!

FOR HOW LONG?!

UNTIL WE SAY SO!

NEVER! I WON'T DO IT! YOU CAN'T MAKE ME!

TH' WAY I SEE IT, YOU BOYS ARE LUCKY TO BE ALIVE!

GRK!

KEEP YOUR VOICES DOWN! WE GOT AWAY FROM TH' VILLAGERS, BUT WE GOT WORSE TROUBLES NOW! THESE WOODS ARE DANGEROUS AT NIGHT!

I WONDER WHAT HAPPENED TO ALL THE RAT CREATURES AFTER THE RACE?

THEY DISAPPEARED INTO TH' FOREST.

FOR ALL WE KNOW, THEY MIGHT BE WATCHING US RIGHT NOW!

AT LEAST I'VE GOT **YOU** BACK, FONE BONE! I'M NEVER LETTING YOU OUT OF MY SIGHT **AGAIN!**

MAYBE FONE BONE'S **DRAGON** WILL PROTECT US.

I HOPE SO. HE ALWAYS HAS BEFORE.

CHILDREN'S STORIES!

I **BEG** YOUR PARDON?

STILL BELIEVE IN **DRAGONS**, DO YOU, BONE? WELL, DON'T WORRY. IF THE HAIRY-MEN **DO** ATTACK, ME AN' ROSIE WILL PROTECT YA.

TH' DRAGON IS **REAL**, LUCIUS! HE'S GOT BIG, DROOPY **EYES**, AN' FLOPPY **EARS** -- ASK GRAN'MA!

UH. . . SOMETHING JUST **MOVED** OVER THERE!

IN TH' WOODS!

MAYBE IT'S THE DRAGON --

shh!

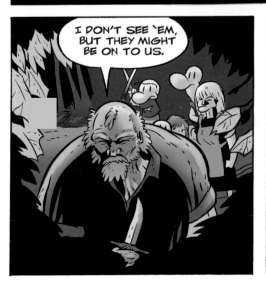

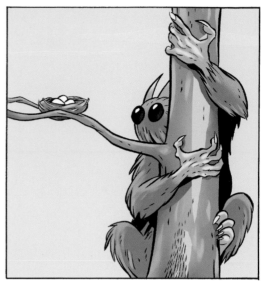

WELL... THE BEAMS ARE SOUND. MOST OF TH' DAMAGE IS TO TH' ROOF.

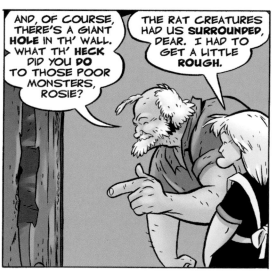

AND, OF COURSE, THERE'S A GIANT HOLE IN TH' WALL. WHAT TH' HECK DID YOU DO TO THOSE POOR MONSTERS, ROSIE?

THE RAT CREATURES HAD US SURROUNDED, DEAR. I HAD TO GET A LITTLE ROUGH.

THIS PLACE LOOKS LIKE A BATTLEFIELD! YOU'RE LUCKY YOU ESCAPED WITH YOUR LIVES!

IT WAS A BIT SCARY, BUT DON'T FORGET I FOUGHT TH' RATS BACK IN TH' BIG WAR!

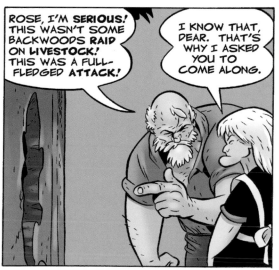

ROSE, I'M SERIOUS! THIS WASN'T SOME BACKWOODS RAID ON LIVESTOCK! THIS WAS A FULL-FLEDGED ATTACK!

I KNOW THAT, DEAR. THAT'S WHY I ASKED YOU TO COME ALONG.

THAT'S **ALSO** WHY I ASKED YOU TO HELP ME RESCUE THE **BONE COUSINS** FROM TH' FOLKS THEY **SWINDLED!**

IT WAS AGAINST **MY BETTER JUDGMENT!** WHY **DID** WE SAVE THEM?

RIGHT NOW, THEY'RE THE **ONLY** CLUE I'VE **GOT.** TH' RAT CREATURES ATTACKED TH' **FARMHOUSE** BECAUSE THEY WERE **LOOKING** FOR THE **BONES!**

I KNEW IT! I KNEW THAT SNEAKY LITTLE RUNT **PHONEY BONE** WAS A **TROUBLEMAKER!!**

HE'S A **TROUBLEMAKER,** ALL RIGHT, BUT I DON'T THINK **HE'S** GOT ANY MORE IDEA ABOUT WHAT'S GOIN' ON THAN **WE DO!**

YOU **DON'T?**

I GRILLED HIS COUSIN **FONE BONE** TH' MORNIN' AFTER THE ATTACK. CLAIMS THEY NEVER EVEN **HEARD** OF RAT CREATURES BEFORE THEY CAME TO OUR VALLEY.

YOU **BELIEVE** HIM?

I **DO.** FONE BONE'S A **GOOD** ONE. AND I THINK HE HAS A **CRUSH** ON THORN!

ISN'T THAT **CUTE?**

HMM. WHAT ABOUT TH' **GOOFY** ONE? SMILEY?

HE HAS NO BRAIN.

NOT ONLY **THAT,** BUT **THORN** THINKS THEY'RE **ALL** INNOCENT! SHE'S A GOOD JUDGE OF CHARACTER, AND I **TRUST** MY GRANDDAUGHTER'S **INTUITION!**

YOU TELLIN' ME **EVERYTHING,** ROSE?

EVERYTHING I **CAN,** SWEETIE.

THEN WHAT ARE WE **DOIN'** HERE? IF THOSE CREATURES COME BACK WITH A BIGGER **WAR PARTY,** WE WON'T BE ABLE TO **HOLD 'EM OFF!**

I KNOW SOMETHING ABOUT TH' WAY RAT CREATURES WORK, AND **MY** GUESS IS THAT THEY'RE GONNA **LAY LOW** FOR A WHILE.

LAY LOW?! THEY ATTACKED TH' COW RACE IN **BROAD DAYLIGHT!!**

THEY DIDN'T ATTACK TH' RACE. **THEY** WERE AS SURPRISED AS **WE WERE!**

I DON'T LIKE IT. WHAT WERE THEY **DOIN'?** WHAT ARE THEY **UP TO?**

IT'S THE **TREATY...** THEY'RE **TESTING** IT. **THAT'S** WHY I HAD TO COME HERE.

ROSE... YOU CAN'T FIGHT 'EM BY YOURSELF.

I'M NOT. THE **DRAGON** IS **BACK.**

SO, LITTLE FONE BONE REALLY **DOES** KNOW ABOUT THE DRAGON!

THORN **DOES**, TOO.

TOLD HER TH' **REST**?

I HAVEN'T DECIDED **WHAT** TO DO, LUCIUS. SHE MIGHT BE IN **MORE** DANGER IF SHE **KNOWS!** SHE HASN'T REACHED THE **TURNING**, YET.

I THINK WE'RE SAFE FOR A WHILE. LET'S WAIT AN' **WATCH** FOR A FEW DAYS...

...THERE'S STILL TH' **POSSIBILITY** THAT THIS IS BETWEEN THE **RAT CREATURES** AND THE **BONES**, AND HAS NOTHING TO **DO** WITH THORN.

IN THE **MEANTIME**, I'M GONNA ENJOY EVERY **MINUTE** OF KEEPIN' THAT RUNT PHONEY BONE **BUSY!**

GOOD. THEN WE CAN START REBUILDING TH' **FARM-HOUSE!**

BUT FIRST, WE BETTER TRY TO GET SOME **SLEEP** WHILE TH' SUN IS OUT!

OKAY, KIDS! LISTEN UP!

WE'RE ALL BEAT FROM TRAVELING ALL NIGHT! LET'S TRY TO GET SOME **SHUT-EYE!**

DID ANYBODY MANAGE TO GET SOME SLEEP ON TH' **ROAD?**

I GOT A LITTLE BIT.

OKAY, BONE. YOU GOT TH' FIRST WATCH.

Dear Thorn,

I know that I am short, bald, and have a big nose,

but I like you a lot!

Signed, a secret admirer XXX OOO

'ROUND AND 'ROUND
   OUR BUSY FEET GO

HURRY AND FURY
   AND APPLE-RED GLOW...

THE SIGHTS AND SOUNDS OF PLACES TO DO...

THE LAUGHING AND SHOUTING WILL NEVER BE THROUGH!

AFTER ALL THAT RUNNING, THE REST IS BEST

AND THE BEST TO REST WITH
IS YOU.

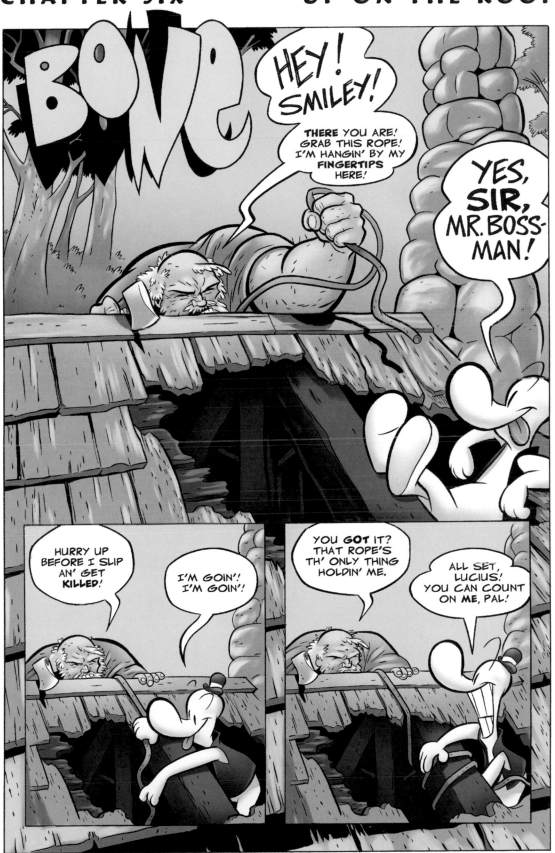

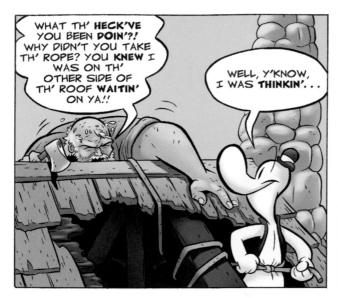

HOLD MY HAT FOR A MINUTE, WILL YA?

WE SHOULD TAKE **ADVANTAGE** OF THIS SOUTHEASTERN EXPOSURE. NOW, I DON'T KNOW ABOUT **YOU**, BUT I'M PICTURING A **GLASSED-IN ATRIUM**. . .

. . . AN' **HERE'S** WHERE WE PUT TH' **JACUZZI!**

BACK IN BONEVILLE YOU WERE TH' **VILLAGE IDIOT**, WEREN'T YOU?

ACTUALLY, I WORKED FOR MY COUSIN **PHONEY**. HE WAS TH' **RICHEST BONE IN BONEVILLE**, BEFORE THEY RAN US OUTTA TOWN. I DIDN'T WORK FOR HIM ALL TH' TIME, THOUGH. JUST KINDA DID **ODD JOBS** FOR HIM WHENEVER HE NEEDED SOMETHIN' DONE.

I USED TO DO THAT FOR A **LOT** OF FOLKS! HELP 'EM OUT. I **LIKE** TO DO THAT. I LIKE TO **HELP** PEOPLE!

TORTURE PEOPLE IS MORE **LIKE** IT.

SIGH.

NOW YOU GOT ME **HOMESICK!** I MISS BONEVILLE!

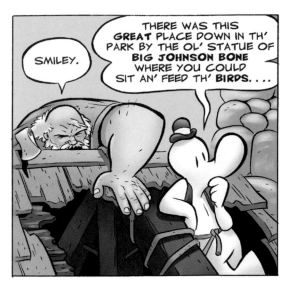

IT AIN'T **BONEVILLE**, BUT IT'LL DO.

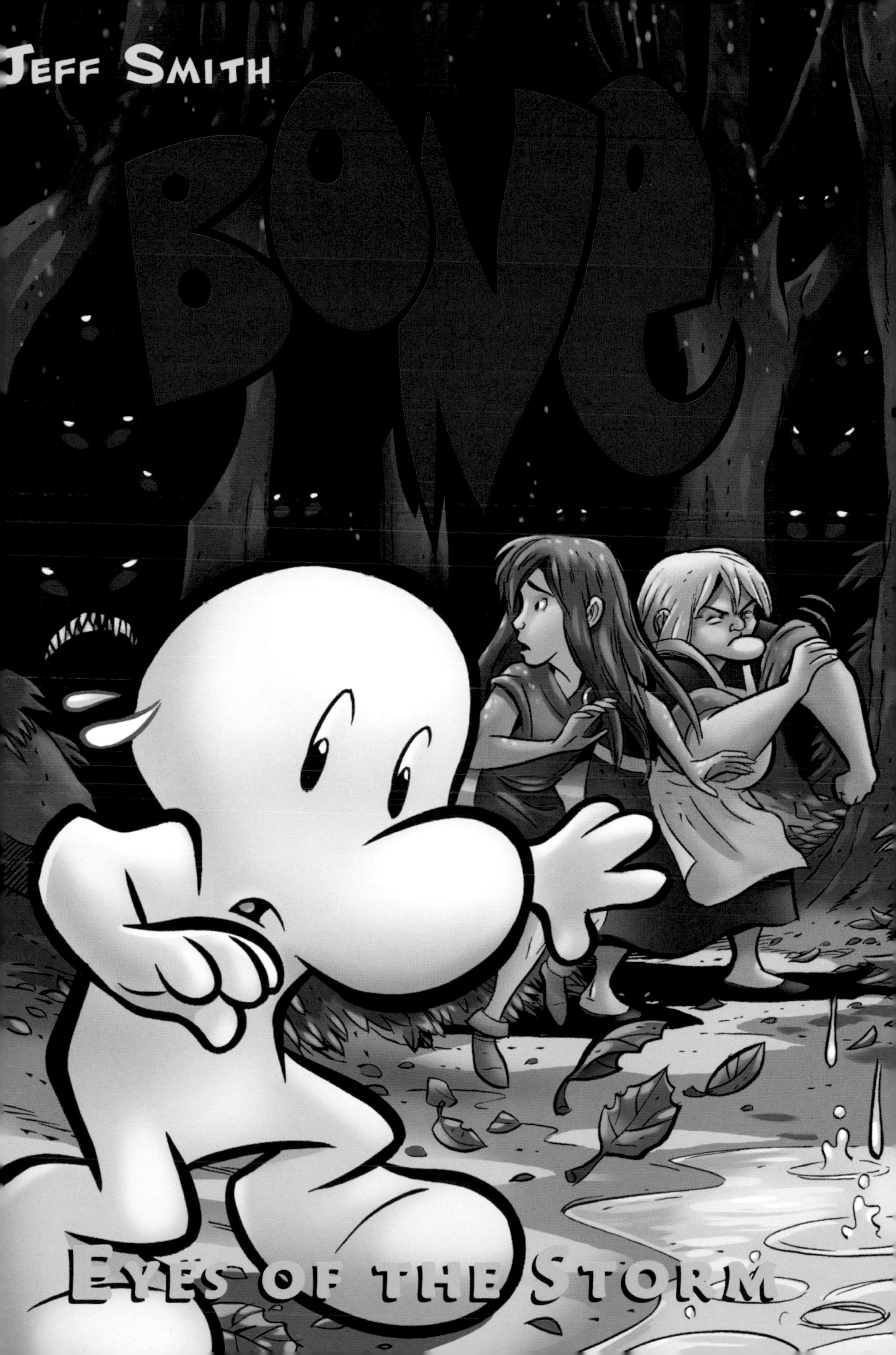
JEFF SMITH
BONE
EYES OF THE STORM

This book is for my parents,

Barbara Goodsell and William Earl Smith

MAYBE I'LL READ IT LATER. SO, WHAT BRINGS YOU BY, MIZ 'POSSUM?

OH, YOU KNOW ME, BONE! I'M ALWAYS CHECKIN' UP ON THINGS -- MAKIN' SURE EVERYBODY'S OKAY!

I SEE YOU BEEN WORKIN' ON TH' FARMHOUSE! HOW'S THAT GOIN'?

WE'RE MAKING PROGRESS. THE RAT CREATURES DID A LOT OF DAMAGE!

OH, I KNOW! ISN'T IT TERRIBLE? AT LEAST YOU PATCHED THAT HOLE IN TH' WALL!

AN' NOT A MOMENT TOO SOON! YOU NEVER KNOW WHEN THOSE HOOLIGANS MIGHT COME BACK!

GRAN'MA THINKS TH' RAT CREATURES WILL STAY AWAY FOR A WHILE.

WELL, YOU'RE PROBABLY ALL RIGHT DURIN' TH' DAYTIME, BUT DON'T TAKE CHANCES AT NIGHT! YOU'RE NOT STILL SLEEPIN' OUTSIDE, ARE YOU?

NO, MA'AM! WE'RE ALL SLEEPIN' INDOORS! IN TH' BIG ROOM DOWNSTAIRS!

AS SOON AS LUCIUS AND SMILEY FINISH THE ROOF, WE'LL MOVE INTO THE BEDROOMS UPSTAIRS.

THAT'S GOOD, ANYWAY...

WATCH DUTY

AN' WHAT ABOUT THAT GREEDY **COUSIN** OF YOURS? **PHONEY BONE**? I HEAR HE CAUSED **QUITE A RUCKUS** AT THAT COW RACE!

GRAN'MA'S MAKIN' HIM SHOVEL OUT TH' BARN...

WITH A SPOON!

SERVES HIM **RIGHT**! WELL, I'D LOVE TO STAY AN' **GOSSIP** ALL DAY, BUT I LEFT TH' **KIDS** WITH MIZ HEDGEHOG, AN' I PROMISED I WOULDN'T BE GONE LONG. HERE, BONE! I BROUGHT THIS FOR YOU!

SILLY ME! I ALMOST FORGOT TO **ASK**... TH' **BOYS** WANTED ME TO FIND OUT HOW YOUR **GRANDMOTHER** DID IN TH' RACE, DEAR!

SHE WON!

THAT'S **WONDERFUL**! OKAY! NOW I REALLY **MUST** BE LEAVING! IF YOU NEED **ANYTHING** AT ALL, YOU JUST **HOLLER**, YOU HEAR?

OH! AND THAT STUFF IN TH' PAN? IF YOU HAVE ANY LEAKS IN THAT **NEW ROOF** OF YOURS - - - -

- - JUST SMEAR THAT **GOO** OVER IT! SEALS UP ANYTHING! GUARANTEED!

THANKS FOR DROPPING BY, MIZ 'POSSUM.

SHE'S RIGHT ABOUT NOT TAKING CHANCES AFTER DARK. WE SHOULD START BACK.

OKAY.

WHOSE TURN IS IT TO STAY UP ON WATCH DUTY?

MINE.

I'LL STAY UP WITH YA IF YA WANT.

YOU SHOULD GET SOME SLEEP. I DON'T MIND STAYING UP BY MYSELF.

BESIDES, AS LONG AS I'M AWAKE, I CAN'T HAVE ANY MORE OF THOSE DREAMS!

DID YOU HAVE ANOTHER WEIRD DREAM?

I HAVEN'T HAD ONE FOR A FEW DAYS NOW, BUT I KEEP WAITING. I'M ALMOST AFRAID TO GO TO SLEEP AT NIGHT!

Y'KNOW, I CAN'T THINK OF A SINGLE DREAM I'VE HAD SINCE I CAME TO THIS VALLEY.

NOT ONE? DO YOU USUALLY REMEMBER YOUR DREAMS?

I ALWAYS REMEMBER MY DREAMS!

HMM. WELL, THINGS ARE A LOT **DIFFERENT** HERE THAN THEY ARE IN **BONEVILLE**! MAYBE YOU JUST NEED SOME TIME TO **ADJUST**.

ME?! **BOY!** I'LL TELL YA WHO NEEDS TO DO A LITTLE **ADJUSTING**! PHONEY BONE!

WHY? HE'S FINALLY STARTING TO **FIT IN** AROUND HERE! AT LEAST HE'S STOPPED COMPLAINING ABOUT HIS **CHORES**!

THAT JUST MEANS HE'S UP TO SOMETHIN'! HE NEVER **LEARNS!**

YOU'RE TOO HARD ON HIM. BACK WHERE **YOU'RE** FROM, PHONEY WAS **WEALTHY!** IMAGINE WHAT IT MUST BE LIKE TO FIND YOURSELF IN A PLACE WHERE **EVERYTHING** YOU VALUE IS COMPLETELY **WORTHLESS!**

YEAH. PHONEY SURE LOVED HIS **MONEY!** WHAT I WOULDN'T HAVE GIVEN TO **SEE HIS FACE** WHEN HE FOUND OUT YOU DON'T **USE** MONEY HERE!

HEH. HIS **JAW** MUST'VE HIT TH' **FLOOR** WHEN HE FIGURED OUT YOUR WHOLE **ECONOMY** IS BASED ON **POULTRY PRODUCTS!**

HE SEEMS TO HAVE ADJUSTED WELL.

YOU'RE **RIGHT!** A LITTLE HONEST WORK, AND **CLEAN, SIMPLE LIVING** WILL DO HIM **GOOD!**

HI, GUYS!

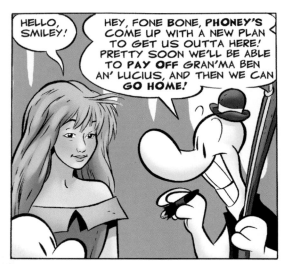

HELLO, SMILEY!

HEY, FONE BONE, *PHONEY'S* COME UP WITH A NEW PLAN TO GET US OUTTA HERE! PRETTY SOON WE'LL BE ABLE TO *PAY OFF* GRAN'MA BEN AN' LUCIUS, AND THEN WE CAN *GO HOME!*

WHAT TH' *HECK* IS *TAKIN'* YOU SO LONG?! *C'MON! C'MON!* YOU GOT ANY *IDEA* HOW *HARD* IT IS TO GET 'EM TO *SIT* IN THOSE LITTLE CHAIRS?!!

ALL SET!

I MISS THAT OL' *THRILL*...

GIMME GIMME GIMME! EGGS! EGGS! EGGS! I'LL BE *RICH!*

HEE HEE HEE HEE HEE HEE HEE HEE *YES!*

OH, YEAH. HE'S ADJUSTED WELL.

I COULD BE WRONG . . .

WATCH DUTY

WASN'T ANYBODY **OUT** THERE, WAS THERE?

NO. BUT THERE **COULD'VE BEEN.**

KINGDOK WILL **NEVER** FIND US! WE'RE **SAFE** HERE! NOW **SHUT UP** AND GO TO SLEEP!

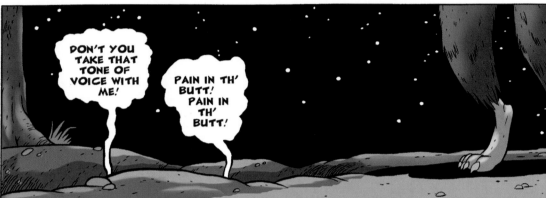

KINGDOK! IT WAS HIS IDEA! I TRIED TO STOP HIM!

IT WAS AN ACCIDENT, SIRE! WE DIDN'T MEAN TO UPSET THE VALLEY CREATURES' COW RACE!

I SHOULD KILL YOU BOTH . . .

BUT YOU KNOW WHAT? I HATE THE FLAT-LANDERS, AND I HATE THE OLD COW WOMAN, AND I REALLY HATE THOSE STUPID COW RACES!

FOR ONCE, YOU TWO MESSED UP, AND I'M HAPPY ABOUT IT!

TH - THEN . . . YOU'RE NOT GOING TO KILL US?

YOU MAY LIVE.

BUT- - BUT WHAT ABOUT TH' HOODED ONE? WE WERE UNDER ORDERS TO LAY LOW!

AM I NOT KINGDOK?! I WILL DISCIPLINE MY TROOPS THE WAY I SEE FIT!!

TAKE THIS!

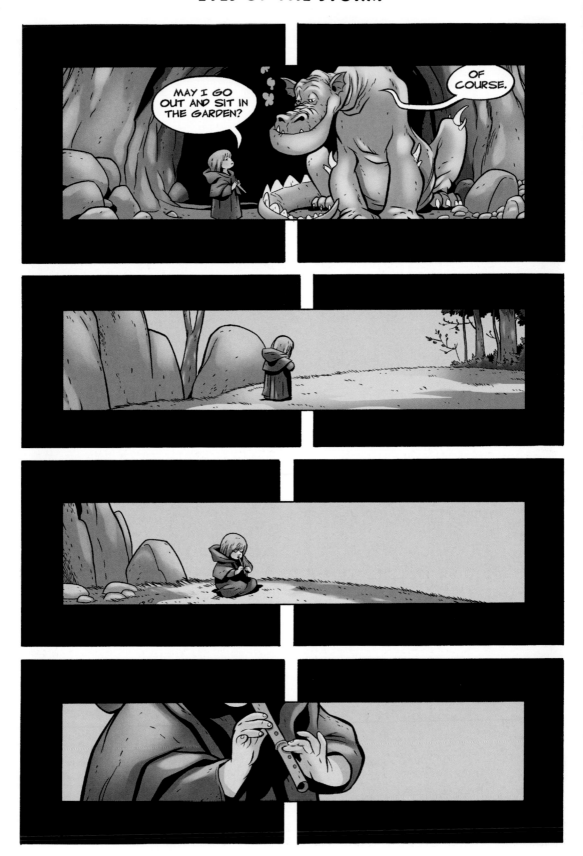

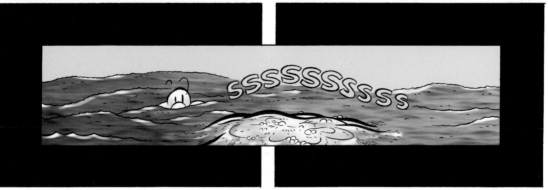

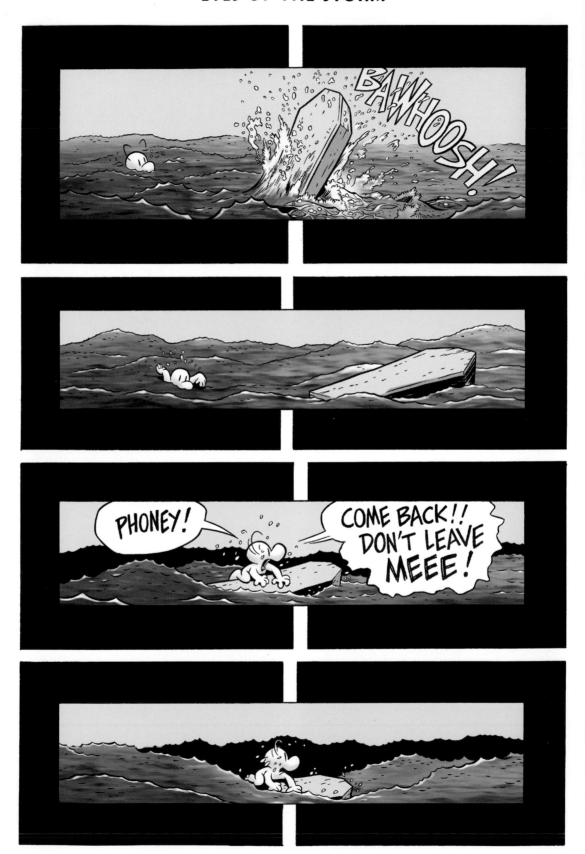

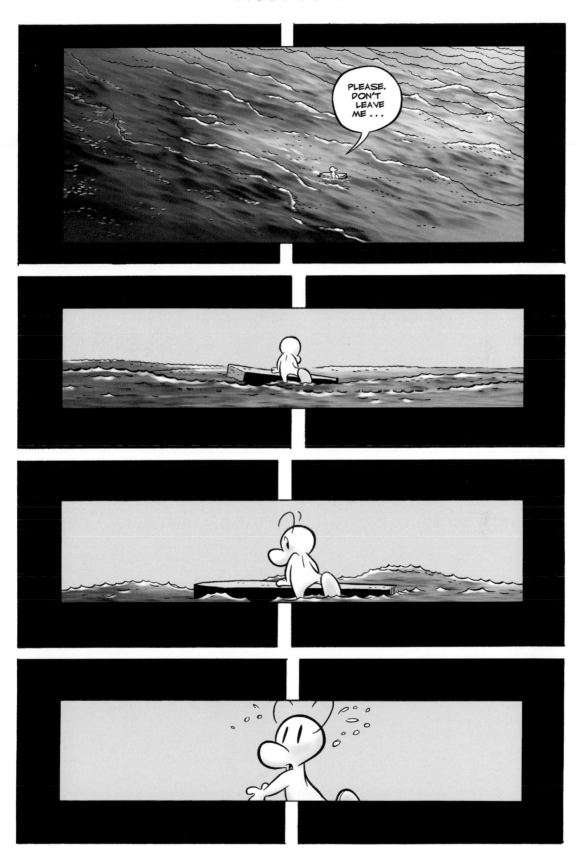

MMMMM.
SNRK!
SNRK!

UNH.

WHOA.

WHERE AM I?

JEEZ! TH' SUN'S BEEN UP FOR **HOURS!**

UH, OH! I OVERSLEPT!

WONDER WHERE EVERYBODY IS? PHONEY?

HELLO?

GRAN'MA? THORN?

HMMM. MUST BE OUT AN' **ABOUT** ALREADY!

HELLO?

HUH! NOBODY'S AROUND!

HIYA, BONE!

HEY, TED! HOW YOU **DOIN'**, YOU OL' **BUG**, YOU?

PURTY GOOD! HOW 'BOUTS YOU? BEEN WORKIN' ON YER **LOVE POETRYS** FOR THORN?

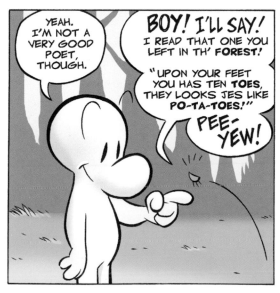

YEAH. I'M NOT A VERY GOOD POET, THOUGH.

BOY! I'LL SAY! I READ THAT ONE YOU LEFT IN TH' **FOREST**! "UPON YOUR FEET YOU HAS TEN **TOES**, THEY LOOKS JES LIKE **PO-TA-TOES!**" **PEE-YEW!**

THAT ONE DOESN'T COUNT! THE **RAT CREATURES** INTERRUPTED ME!

YOU OUGHTA **THANK 'EM!** THEY DID YOU A **FLAVOR!**

NOW TO FIND A NICE, **QUIET** SPOT TO WRITE!

PREFERABLY SOMEPLACE **PRIVATE!**

THIS LOOKS *GOOD!* A SUN-DRENCHED MEADOW **BESPECKLED** WITH **WILD FLOWERS**, AN' TH' **AIR** FILLED WITH **WAFTED SCENTS** OF **HONEYSUCKLE** AN' **MARIGOLDS!**

YEAH, YEAH! THIS IS TH' **PERFECT** PLACE TO WORK ON MY **ULTIMATE** EXPRESSION OF LOVE FOR THORN! LET'S SEE . . . A **ROSE** IS A ROSE IS A . . . HUM TE DUM . . .

. . . A **ROSE!** RIGHT!

♪ HMM, HMM, MMMM. HMMM. ♪

OH, *YES!* THIS IS GOOD! THIS IS **REAL** GOOD!

I WONDER WHAT RHYMES WITH **SMOOTH, BROWN THIGH?**

HI, FONE BONE! WHATCHA WORKIN' ON?

HOW TH' **HECK** DID HE KNOW I WAS **ISHMAEL** IN THAT DREAM? THAT'S **IMPOSSIBLE!** IT'S A **COINCIDENCE!**

DON'T THINK ABOUT IT.

NOW, WHERE WAS I?

A ROSE IS A ROSE IS A ROSE . . .

OH, **YEAH!** MY MASTERPIECE!

HMM, HMM.

HOWDY, FONE BONE! FINALLY GOT UP, I SEE!

HEY, GUYS. WHATCHA UP TO?

AS LITTLE AS WE CAN GET **AWAY** WITH! WHAT'RE **YOU** DOIN'? WRITIN' SOMETHIN'?

ME? NO.

LEMME SEE THAT!

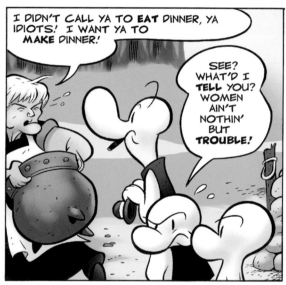

I WANT YOU BOYS TO CATCH YOURSELVES **FOUR CHICKENS!** WHEN SMILEY'S GOT THAT WATER GOIN' **NICE AN' HOT,** DIP TH' **BIRDS** IN IT! I WANT EVERY ONE OF THEM **FEATHERS** GONE, SO **SOAK** 'EM **GOOD!** I BETTER BE SMELLIN' **WET FEATHERS** BACK HERE!

POO! THERE'S A SMELL YOU DON'T FORGET TOO **QUICK!**

OHMYGOSH.

WE'RE GONNA **BOIL** 'EM **ALIVE?!**

OF COURSE NOT, DEAR. YOU'RE GONNA **CUT** THEIR HEADS OFF FIRST.

WITH WHAT?

WITH TH' HATCHET.

UH . . .

ARE THEY GONNA . . . Y'KNOW . . . RUN AROUND TH' **YARD?** SQUIRTIN' **BLOOD** AN' STUFF?

WHAT'S TH' MATTER? AIN'T YOU BOYS EVER CHOPPED TH' HEAD OFF A **CHICKEN** BEFORE?

UH . . .

UH . . .

OH, FER HEAVEN'S SAKES! IF YA CAN'T HANDLE A LITTLE **FLAPPIN' AROUND,** JUST GRAB TH' CHICKEN BY TH' **NECK** AN' GIVE HER A GOOD **CRANK** OVER YOUR HEAD -- THAT'LL **KILL** HER FIRST!

THIS IS ALL **YOUR** FAULT, YOU KNOW. IF YOU'D **WON** THAT STUPID **COW RACE** I'D BE **RICH** RIGHT NOW, INSTEAD OF WASHIN' **DISHES** FOR **BIGFOOT** OVER THERE!

NOBODY **ASKED** YOU TO CLIMB INTO TH' COW SUIT WITH ME.

WHAT **ELSE** WAS I GONNA DO?! I CAN'T TRUST **YOU** TO DO ANYTHING RIGHT!!

BALLAST! THAT'S ALL YOU WERE!

B-A-L-A-S-S-T!

KNOCK IT OFF! YOU TWO BETTER NOT CRAP AROUND LIKE THIS TH' WHOLE WAY TO BARRELHAVEN! NOW, C'MON, LET'S GO!

YEAH, YEAH. ARE WE GONNA EAT BREAKFAST FIRST, OR WHAT?

WE'LL EAT ON TH' ROAD.

HAPPINESS ABOUNDING! ROAD RATIONS! I **LOVE** THOSE HARD, STALE, STUFFED **BREAD** THINGIES!

HOW DID **YOU** SLEEP LAST NIGHT, FONE BONE?

I DIDN'T HAVE ANY MORE WEIRD DREAMS. WHAT ABOUT YOU?

EVERYBODY OUTSIDE! MOVE IT! MOVE IT!

I SLEPT PRETTY HARD. NO NEW DREAMS FOR ME, EITHER.

RRRR.

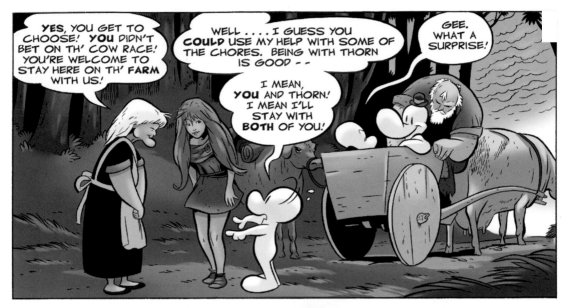

YES, YOU GET TO CHOOSE! **YOU** DIDN'T BET ON TH' COW RACE! YOU'RE WELCOME TO STAY HERE ON TH' **FARM** WITH US!

WELL .... I GUESS YOU **COULD** USE MY HELP WITH SOME OF THE CHORES. BEING WITH THORN IS GOOD --

GEE. WHAT A SURPRISE!

I MEAN, **YOU** AND THORN! I MEAN I'LL STAY WITH **BOTH** OF YOU!

GOOD-BYE, BOYS! KEEP A SHARP LOOKOUT ON TH' ROAD!

WE'LL BE BACK IN A FEW DAYS, ROSE. TAKE CARE OF YOURSELF.

SEE YA LATER, GUYS!

BITE ME.

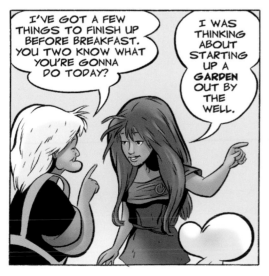

I'VE GOT A FEW THINGS TO FINISH UP BEFORE BREAKFAST. YOU TWO KNOW WHAT YOU'RE GONNA DO TODAY?

I WAS THINKING ABOUT STARTING UP A **GARDEN** OUT BY THE WELL.

THAT'S A **FINE** IDEA! BUT FEED TH' **CHICKENS** FIRST!

OKAY! C'MON, FONE BONE!

REALLY?!

IT WAS A **LONG** TIME AGO.... SHE WAS A **BEAUTIFUL** WOMAN -- TH' MOST BEAUTIFUL WOMAN IN TH' WHOLE VALLEY ...

WE WERE IN LOVE, AND WE COURTED. A LOT OF FOLKS THOUGHT WE WERE GONNA GET HITCHED...

SO WHAT **HAPPENED?** WHY DIDN'T YOU GET MARRIED?

SHE DIDN'T WANT TO.

HMM. THAT STORM IS BLOWIN' IN A LOT FASTER THAN I THOUGHT.

UH, OH!

WE GOT TROUBLE!

THERE'S SOMEONE **FOLLOWING US!**

WARD OFF WHAT?

DON'T YOU KNOW WHAT A GHOST CIRCLE IS?

NO.

HAVE YOU EVER WALKED IN THE WOODS AT NIGHT AND COME ACROSS A **COLD** SPOT? AND SUDDENLY A **CHILL** RUNS UP YOUR SPINE?

YEAH . . . I THINK I HAVE.

THAT'S A GHOST CIRCLE!

THEY'RE SUPPOSED TO BE OPENINGS TO THE **SPIRIT WORLD**. I GUESS IN THE OLD DAYS, THEY WERE PRETTY DANGEROUS.

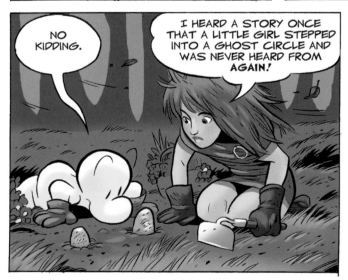

NO KIDDING.

I HEARD A STORY ONCE THAT A LITTLE GIRL STEPPED INTO A GHOST CIRCLE AND WAS NEVER HEARD FROM AGAIN!

PLINK!

WHAT DO I DO? WHAT DO I DO?

WALK YOUR COW OVER TO US . . . BUT DO IT **SLOWLY**. DON'T MAKE ANY SUDDEN MOVES.

HERE. TAKE THIS KNIFE AN' KEEP YER HEAD DOWN . . . I'M GONNA TRY TO STALL 'EM SO SMILEY CAN GET PAST US . . .

HAIRY MEN!

WHY HAVE YOU STOPPED US?!

SSSSSSS

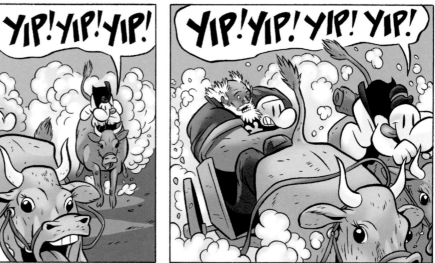

DREAMS ARE WINDOWS TO THE SPIRIT WORLD...

THAT'S WHAT OUR ANCESTORS BELIEVED.

A WORLD FROM WHICH EVERYONE COMES...

...AND TO WHICH EVERYONE MUST ONE DAY RETURN.

IN THE OLD TIMES, IT WAS BELIEVED OUR ANCESTORS COULD MOVE THROUGH THE SPIRIT WORLD AND VISIT OTHER PEOPLE'S DREAMS.

DO YOU AND GRAN'MA BELIEVE THAT?

I'M NOT SURE. GRAN'MA NEVER LIKED TO TALK ABOUT DREAMS. ESPECIALLY **MY** DREAMS ABOUT **DRAGONS**.

WELL, I DON'T KNOW ANYTHING ABOUT **SPIRIT WORLDS**, BUT IT SURE **SEEMS** LIKE THE DRAGON PAID ME A VISIT THE OTHER NIGHT...

HIS **HEAD** APPEARED IN MY DREAM BREAKING THROUGH THE SURFACE OF THE OCEAN... WHEN I TOLD HIM ABOUT IT THE NEXT DAY, **HE** SAYS, **WELCOME ABOARD, ISHMAEL!**

ONLY THE **WEIRD** THING IS I NEVER TOLD HIM THE DREAM WAS ABOUT **MOBY DICK!**

HE SAID **ISHMAEL**? HE **KNEW** YOUR DREAM WAS ABOUT MOBY DICK?

SCARY, HUH? HOW'D HE KNOW WHAT I WAS DREAMING ABOUT?

AND HE KNEW ABOUT THAT CREEPY GUY IN **YOUR** DREAM, TOO! SO WHO WAS **THAT**?

IN **MY** DREAM? I DON'T KNOW . . .

IT WAS A HOODED FIGURE. WHOEVER -- OR WHATEVER -- IT WAS, I WAS VERY FRIGHTENED.

HM. AND YOU SAID HE HAD MY FACE.

HE HAD YOUR FACE, BUT I THINK . . . HE WAS JUST USING IT TO **LURE** ME TO HIM.

AND A **GROUP** OF HOODED PEOPLE WERE TAKING YOU OVER THE MOUNTAINS TO LIVE WITH THE **DRAGONS** . . .

YES. THAT WAS THE DREAM I USED TO HAVE AS A LITTLE GIRL.

I WONDER HOW **SAFE** IT IS FOR US TO BE **TALKING** ABOUT THIS . . .

ALL THE DREAMS ARE ABOUT **DRAGONS** AND **HOODED PEOPLE**! THERE'S A **PATTERN** HERE, THORN! SOMETHING'S GOING ON!

DID YOU **HEAR** SOMETHING?

GRAN'MA BEN KNOWS THE TRUTH ABOUT WHERE YOU WERE **RAISED**! HOW COME **SHE'S** NEVER TOLD YOU? INSTEAD, **SHE** TOLD YOU THAT DRAGONS AREN'T **REAL** --

CREEAK

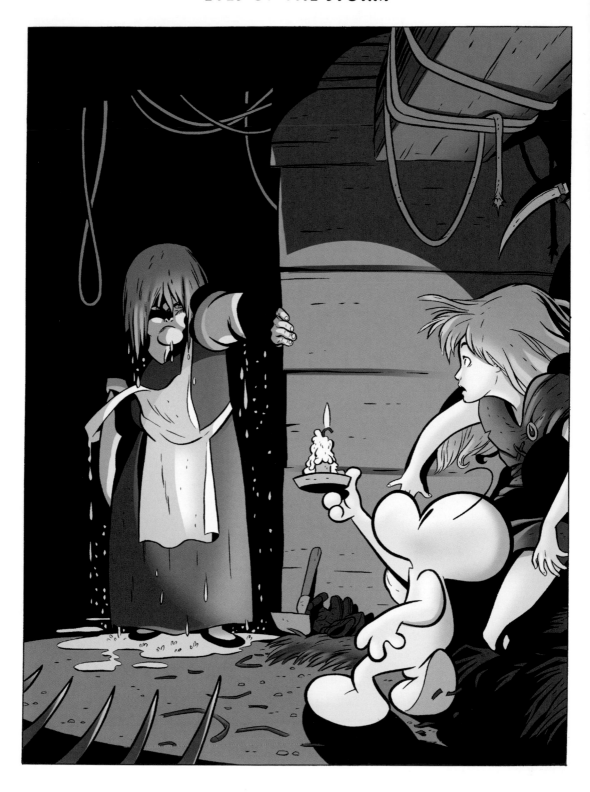

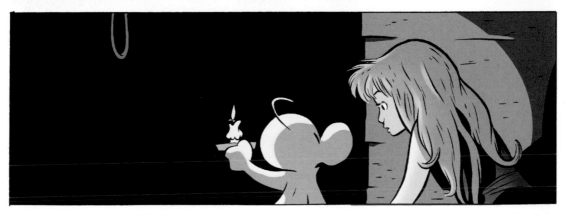

WHAT TH' HECK WAS **THAT** ALL ABOUT?!

I DON'T KNOW. SHE LOOKED **REALLY** UPSET.

DO YOU THINK SHE OVERHEARD US TALKING ABOUT OUR **DREAMS?**

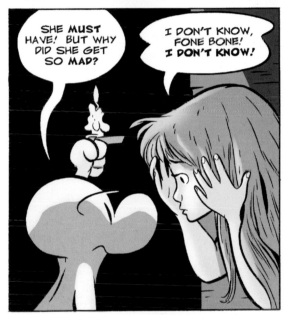

SHE **MUST** HAVE! BUT WHY DID SHE GET SO MAD?

I DON'T KNOW, FONE BONE! **I DON'T KNOW!**

WELL, **I** DO! SOMEONE'S BEEN PLAYIN' AROUND IN OUR **HEADS** GIVIN' US **NIGHTMARES,** AN' YOUR **GRANDMOTHER** KNOWS SOMETHIN' **ABOUT IT!**

C'MON! WE GOTTA CATCH HER!

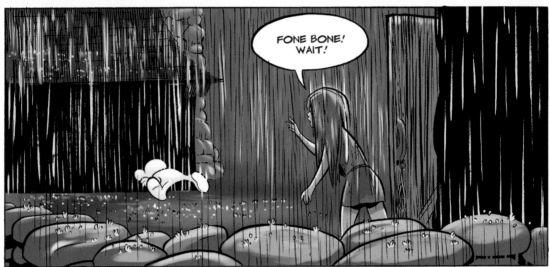

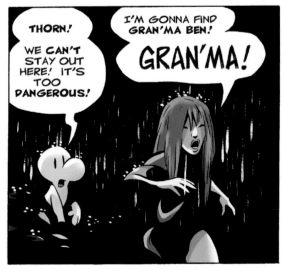

GRAN'MA!

YOU SCARED US HALF TO **DEATH!** ARE YOU OKAY?

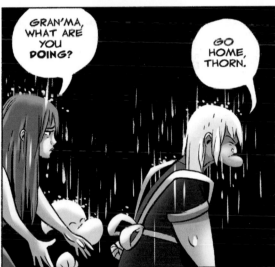

GRAN'MA, WHAT ARE YOU **DOING?**

GO HOME, THORN.

I'M NOT GOING BACK WITHOUT YOU!

AN' I'M NOT GOIN' BACK UNTIL YOU TELL US WHAT'S GOIN' ON!

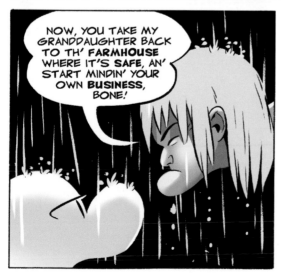

FIRST YOU COME SNEAKIN' INTO TH' BARN TO LISTEN IN ON OUR CONVERSATION, THEN YOU GO CHARGIN' OFF IN TH' WOODS LIKE A CRAZY PERSON!

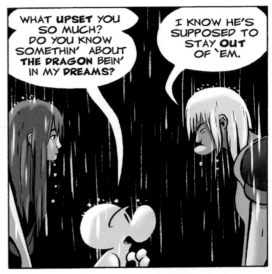

WHAT UPSET YOU SO MUCH? DO YOU KNOW SOMETHIN' ABOUT THE DRAGON BEIN' IN MY DREAMS?

I KNOW HE'S SUPPOSED TO STAY OUT OF 'EM.

WHAT?

GO BACK TO TH' HOUSE! THESE WOODS ARE DANGEROUS!

YOU'RE GOING TO SEE HIM RIGHT NOW, AREN'T YOU? YOU'RE GOING TO SEE THE DRAGON!

WHAT DO YOU MEAN HE'S SUPPOSED TO STAY OUT OF MY DREAMS?

FOR TH' LAST TIME, BONE, GET BACK TO TH' HOUSE BEFORE - -

KEERAAK BOOM!

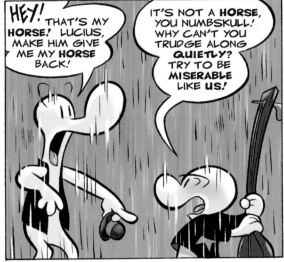

YOU MISSED YOUR **BIG CHANCE**, LUCIUS! YOU COULDA HANDED ME OVER TO 'EM! WHY **DIDN'T** YA?

'CAUSE YOU OWE ME A **LOTTA EGGS** . . .

. . . AND I'M **REALLY** LOOKIN' FORWARD TO BUSTIN' YOUR CHOPS ALL **SUMMER LONG!**

YOU'LL BE **THANKIN'** ME BY TH' END OF TH' SUMMER! AT LEAST WITH **ME** THERE, THAT TWO-BIT JOINT HAS A CHANCE TO TURN A PROFIT!

OH! OH! NOW YOU GOT SOMETHIN' TO SAY ABOUT TH' WAY I RUN MY **BAR?!**

OH, **PLEASE!** DON'T EVEN GET ME **STARTED!**

YOU THINK YOU CAN RUN THE **BARRELHAVEN TAVERN** BETTER THAN I CAN?

YOU WOULDN'T KNOW A **BOTTOM LINE** IF IT JUMPED UP AN' TUGGED YA ON TH' **BEARD!**

CARE TO MAKE A LITTLE **WAGER** ON THAT?

DOUBLE OR NOTHING

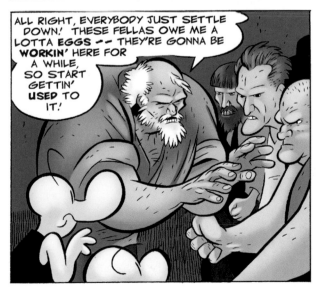

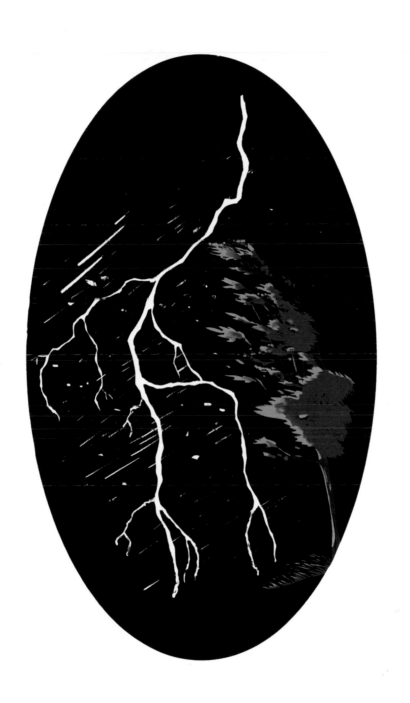

BOOM KABABOOM

BONE. GET YOUR HEAD OVER BY THAT TREE AN' TAKE A LOOK AROUND.

EYES OF THE STORM

GRAN'MA?

DO YOU THINK THE RAT CREATURES SAW US? MAYBE THEY DON'T KNOW WE'RE HERE.

THEY KNOW.

AN' IT WON'T BE LONG BEFORE THEY **FIND US,** EITHER.

I WISH YOU TWO HADN'T FOLLOWED ME OUT HERE.

WE WERE WORRIED ABOUT **YOU!**

WE WERE WORRIED YOU MIGHT DO SOMETHING **CRAZY!** LIKE RUN OUT HERE AN' PICK A **FIGHT** WITH TH' **DRAGON!**

THAT'S ENOUGH!

WHY ARE YOU SO **MAD** AT HIM?

I DON'T WANNA HEAR ANOTHER **WORD** OUT OF **YOU**, BONE! THIS WHOLE THING IS **YOUR** FAULT!

GRAN'MA! THAT'S NOT **TRUE**!

KEEP STILL, THORN! EVERYTHING WAS UNDER CONTROL UNTIL HE CAME TO OUR VALLEY AND **WOKE THE DRAGON**!

YOU KNOW MORE ABOUT THE DRAGON THAN HE DOES!

WHAT **I** KNOW ABOUT TH' DRAGON IS MY — —

HOLD IT.

GET DOWN.

GET DOWN. GET DOWN.

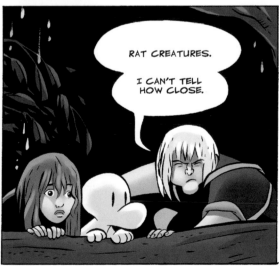

RAT CREATURES.

I CAN'T TELL HOW CLOSE.

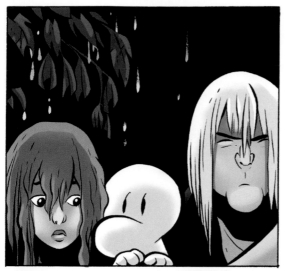

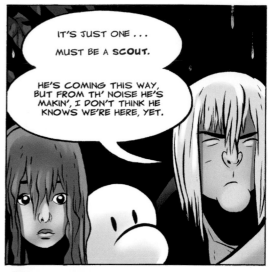

IT'S JUST ONE . . . MUST BE A **SCOUT**.

HE'S COMING THIS WAY, BUT FROM TH' NOISE HE'S MAKIN', I DON'T THINK HE KNOWS WE'RE HERE, YET.

I'M GOIN' OUT THERE.

I WANT YOU TO **SIT** HERE AND NOT MOVE A **MUSCLE!** DO YOU UNDERSTAND ME?

DO YOU?!

YES.

UH, HUH.

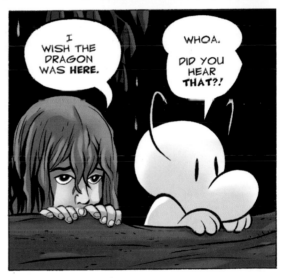

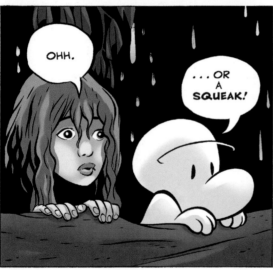

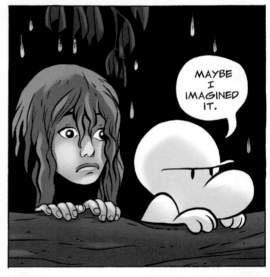

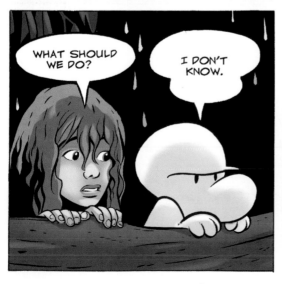

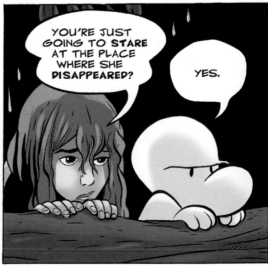

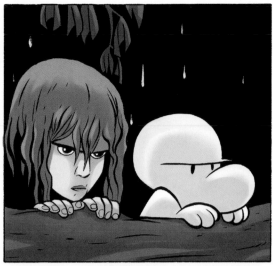

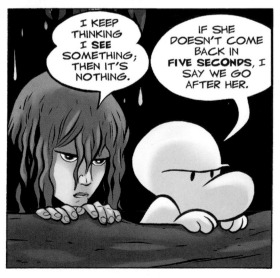

I KEEP THINKING I **SEE** SOMETHING; THEN IT'S NOTHING.

IF SHE DOESN'T COME BACK IN **FIVE SECONDS**, I SAY WE GO AFTER HER.

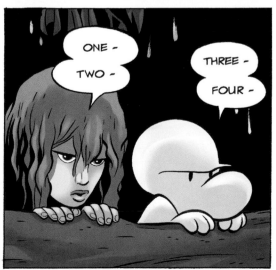

ONE -

TWO -

THREE -

FOUR -

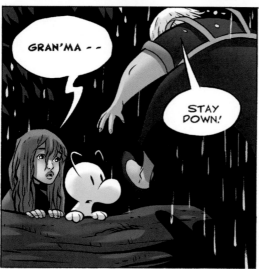

GRAN'MA --

STAY DOWN!

IT'S BAD.

TH' FOREST IS **SWARMING** WITH RAT CREATURES, AND THEY'RE MOVIN' **THIS WAY!**

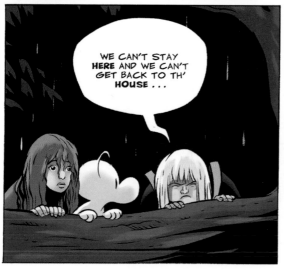

WE CAN'T STAY **HERE** AND WE CAN'T GET BACK TO TH' HOUSE . . .

WE'RE GONNA HAFTA **OUTRUN** 'EM.

KEERAAKOW!

THE DRAGON!

IT'S THE DRAGON!

HE CAME! AN' HE CHASED OFF TH' RAT CREATURES! WE'RE SAFE NOW!!

GET BEHIND TH' TREE.

GRAN'MA!
THE DRAGON JUST
SAVED OUR
LIVES!
LEAVE HIM
ALONE!

GRAN'MA?

PLEASE?

SIGH

KRAAAKKLE

I'M SO TIRED, BONE.

THANK YOU, GRAN'MA.

YOU THINK TH' DRAGON'LL BE THERE WHENEVER YOU **NEED** HIM . . .

. . . WELL, HE WON'T BE.

HE WASN'T ALWAYS THERE FOR ME.

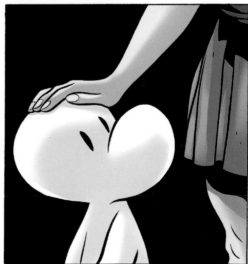

GRAN'MA BEN?

CAN WE TALK TO YOU?

TALK AWAY.

I CAN LISTEN AN' MEND FENCES AT TH' SAME TIME.

AREN'T THOSE FENCES KINDA **SMALL** FOR KEEPIN' OUT **RAT CREATURES?**

THESE ARE **COW FENCES,** BONE. BUT I'M **FIXIN'** 'EM TO LET THE MONSTERS KNOW WHERE TH' **BOUNDARIES** ARE!

CHUNK

GRAN'MA — —

JUST A MOMENT, THORN. THERE'S SOMETHIN' I HAVE TO SAY TO FONE BONE . . .

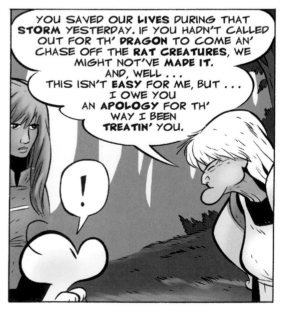

YOU SAVED OUR **LIVES** DURING THAT **STORM** YESTERDAY. IF YOU HADN'T CALLED OUT FOR TH' **DRAGON** TO COME AN' CHASE OFF THE **RAT CREATURES,** WE MIGHT NOT'VE **MADE IT.** AND, WELL . . . THIS ISN'T **EASY** FOR ME, BUT . . . I OWE YOU AN **APOLOGY** FOR TH' WAY I BEEN **TREATIN'** YOU.

!

OH, NO, GRAN'MA. YOU DON'T OWE ME ANYTHING . . .

YES, I **DO**. EVER SINCE YOU **CAME** TO OUR VALLEY, I'VE BEEN **SUSPICIOUS** OF YOU AN' YOUR COUSINS . . .

I'VE **BLAMED** YOU BOYS FOR ALL THE RAT CREATURE ATTACKS AN' EVERYTHING **ELSE** THAT'S GONE WRONG . . .

. . . AN' IN PARTICULAR, I BLAMED **YOU** FOR DISTURBING TH' **DRAGON**.

TRUTH **IS**, OUR TROUBLES HERE IN TH' **VALLEY** STARTED A LONG TIME BEFORE **YOU** GOT HERE.

APOLOGY ACCEPTED, GRAN'MA.

GRAN'MA . . . FONE BONE HAS SOMETHING IN HIS **KNAPSACK** THAT I WANT HIM TO SHOW YOU.

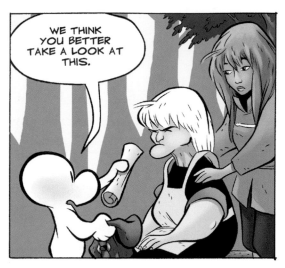

WE THINK YOU BETTER TAKE A LOOK AT THIS.

WHAT TH' **HECK** IS IT?

JUST READ IT.

UM . . . FONE BONE, THIS ISN'T THE - -

My heart beats for you, my pookie so true... I love you so **MUCHer** and **MUCHess**...

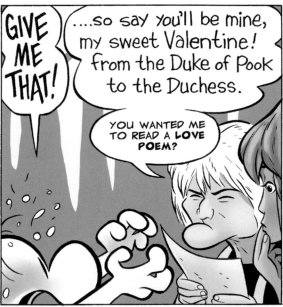

GIVE ME THAT!

....so say you'll be mine, my sweet Valentine! from the Duke of Pook to the Duchess.

YOU WANTED ME TO READ A **LOVE** POEM?

THAT'S **NOT** TH' RIGHT THING! **HERE! HERE!** **THIS** IS IT! IT'S A **MAP!**

JEEZ!

THIS IS A **MAP**?! IT'S SO **FADED** I CAN'T MAKE **HEADS OR TAILS** OUTTA THIS THING!

IT'S IN PRETTY BAD SHAPE. WE FOUND IT OUT IN TH' **DESERT**. LOOK! YOU CAN STILL MAKE OUT TH' **MOUNTAINS** AN' TH' **WATERFALL**! SEE? IT'S A MAP OF THIS **VALLEY**!

LOOKS LIKE IT WAS DRAWN BY A **FIVE-YEAR-OLD**!

IT WAS . . .

I DREW THAT MAP WHEN I WAS IN **DEREN GARD** WITH THE **DRAGONS**.

DON'T SAY ANOTHER WORD! THE FOREST HAS **EARS**!

INSIDE.

QUICKLY.

WELL?

WHERE DID YOU SAY YOU FOUND THAT **MAP**?

MY COUSINS AN' I FOUND IT AFTER WE GOT RUN OUTTA **BONEVILLE!**

WE WERE **LOST** OUT IN TH' **DESERT** AN' **SMILEY BONE** FOUND IT RIGHT BEFORE TH' **LOCUSTS** CAME AN' **SEPARATED** US!

LOCUSTS.

YES, MA'AM

WELL, NOW . . .

LOCUSTS. THAT'S — —

HMM. LET'S **THINK** ABOUT THIS . . .

IT CAN'T MEAN **THAT** ANYMORE . . .

WHAT? **WHAT** CAN'T IT MEAN?!

GRAN'MA! IT'S TIME TO TELL US **THE TRUTH!**

FONE BONE . . . BE A DEAR -- RUN AND FETCH ME A DRINK OF WATER . . .

YES, MA'AM.

GRANDMOTHER, I'M WAITING.

YES.

YES, OF COURSE YOU ARE . . .

. . . IT'S JUST SO DIFFICULT TO KNOW WHERE TO START.

LET'S START WITH MY **DREAMS** . . .

YOU TOLD ME DRAGONS WERE **MAKE-BELIEVE**, BUT YOU **KNEW** THAT WASN'T TRUE!

I HAD NOWHERE ELSE TO TURN.

AFTER YOUR PARENTS DIED, I **HAD** TO HIDE YOU WITH THE DRAGONS.

THE TWO OF US NEEDED TO DISAPPEAR.

THE DRAGONS KEPT YOU SAFE WHILE I SEARCHED FOR A SMALL TOWN WHERE NO ONE WOULD RECOGNIZE US.

WHY?

FOR YOUR SAFETY, CHILD.

WHY DID YOU **LIE** TO ME?!

WHY DID YOU TELL ME THAT IT NEVER **HAPPENED**?! THAT **DRAGONS** DON'T EVEN **EXIST**?!!

I WAS TRYING TO PROTECT YOU. I WAS TRYING TO PROTECT THE **WHOLE VALLEY**.

I CAN'T BELIEVE THIS.

I HAD A LOT OF **RESPONSIBILITIES** IN THOSE DAYS.

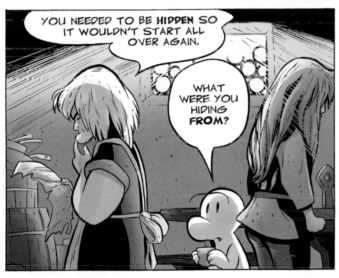

YOU NEEDED TO BE **HIDDEN** SO IT WOULDN'T START ALL OVER AGAIN.

WHAT WERE YOU HIDING **FROM**?

DON'T RUSH ME, BONE. I'M NOT TOO FOND OF DISCUSSING **FAMILY MATTERS** AS IT IS.

IT STARTED BACK IN THE **BIG WAR** . . .

WE WERE FIGHTING THE RAT CREATURES OVER WHO OWNED THE VALLEY.

WE HAD IT AND THEY **WANTED** IT.

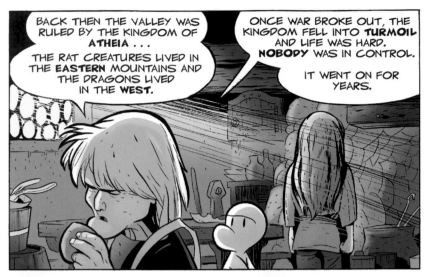

BACK THEN THE VALLEY WAS RULED BY THE KINGDOM OF **ATHEIA** . . . THE RAT CREATURES LIVED IN THE **EASTERN** MOUNTAINS AND THE DRAGONS LIVED IN THE **WEST**.

ONCE WAR BROKE OUT, THE KINGDOM FELL INTO **TURMOIL** AND LIFE WAS HARD. **NOBODY** WAS IN CONTROL.

IT WENT ON FOR YEARS.

FAMILIES FELL APART AND WE ALL LOST FRIENDS.

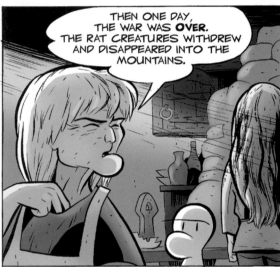

THEN ONE DAY, THE WAR WAS **OVER**. THE RAT CREATURES WITHDREW AND DISAPPEARED INTO THE MOUNTAINS.

WE KNEW THEY'D BE BACK -- BUT WHEN THEY **DID** COME BACK, SOMETHING HAD **CHANGED**. THEIR NEW ATTACKS WERE MUCH MORE **VICIOUS**.

ATTACKS SO FAST AND **BRUTAL** THEY BECAME KNOWN AS **THE NIGHTS OF LIGHTNING**.

I WAS UP HERE IN THE NORTH, TRYING TO WORK AN ALLIANCE BETWEEN **DRAGONS** AND **MEN**, WHEN I HEARD THE NEWS . . .

ATHEIA HAD FALLEN AND ALL OF THE ROYAL FAMILY HAD BEEN KILLED.

SLOWLY, WITH THE HELP OF THE **DRAGONS**, WE FORCED THE RATS OUT OF THE VALLEY AND A **TREATY** WAS SIGNED . . . THE RATS AGREED TO STAY IN THE **MOUNTAINS**, AND THE VALLEY PEOPLE AGREED **NOT TO REBUILD THE KINGDOM**.

OKAY, BUT WHY DID YOU HAVE TO HIDE **THORN**?

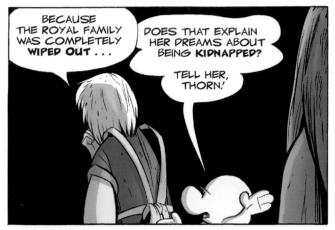

BECAUSE THE ROYAL FAMILY WAS COMPLETELY **WIPED OUT** . . .

DOES THAT EXPLAIN HER DREAMS ABOUT BEING **KIDNAPPED**?

TELL HER, THORN.'

IN ONE OF MY DREAMS - - - I AM TAKEN OVER THE MOUNTAINS AT NIGHT BY PEOPLE WHOSE FACES I CANNOT **SEE** . . .

. . . THEY HAVE **HOODS** PULLED DOWN OVER THEIR FACES.

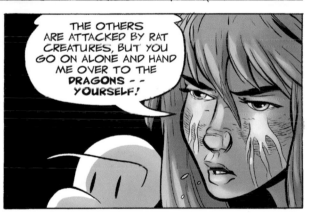

GRAN'MA, I THINK ONE OF THEM IS **YOU**.

THEN, SOMEWHERE **HIGH** IN THE MOUNTAINS, WE ARE **BETRAYED**!

THE OTHERS ARE ATTACKED BY RAT CREATURES, BUT YOU GO ON ALONE AND HAND ME OVER TO THE **DRAGONS** - - **YOURSELF**!

I THINK YOU SHOULD SIT DOWN.

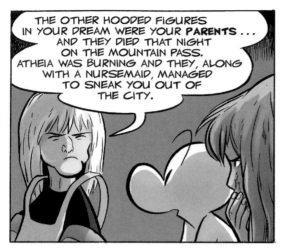

THE OTHER HOODED FIGURES IN YOUR DREAM WERE YOUR **PARENTS** . . . AND THEY DIED THAT NIGHT ON THE MOUNTAIN PASS. ATHEIA WAS BURNING AND THEY, ALONG WITH A NURSEMAID, MANAGED TO SNEAK YOU OUT OF THE CITY.

GO ON.

TRAVELING ONLY AT NIGHT, AND IN COMPLETE SECRECY, THEY MANAGED TO MAKE THEIR WAY **NORTH** ALONG THE FOOTHILLS OF THE MOUNTAINS TO THE PASS CALLED **THE DRAGON'S STAIR.**

I MET THE ROYAL PARTY THERE ON THE PASS . . .

I WAS ESCORTING THEM TO THE DRAGONS' STRONGHOLD IN **DEREN GARD** WHEN WE WERE **BETRAYED!**

A BAND OF **RAT CREATURES** LED BY THEIR CHIEFTAIN **KINGDOK** APPEARED IN THE PASS BEHIND US. YOUR PARENTS CHOSE TO STAY AND **FIGHT** THE MONSTERS WHILE I WENT ON TO DELIVER YOU TO THE **GREAT RED DRAGON.**

IT WAS THE **NURSEMAID** WHO BETRAYED US.

I RUSHED BACK, BUT THE **MASSACRE** WAS OVER. NO ONE WAS LEFT ALIVE. EVEN THE TRAITOROUS MAID WAS TORN IN TWO.

YOUR FATHER WAS **DEAD** . . . KILLED BY THE RAT CREATURES.

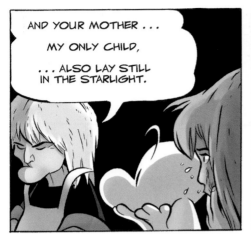

AND YOUR MOTHER . . .
MY ONLY CHILD,
. . . ALSO LAY STILL IN THE STARLIGHT.

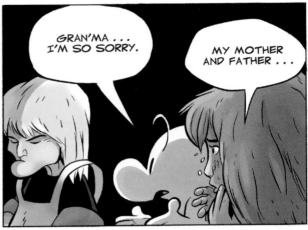

GRAN'MA . . . I'M SO SORRY.

MY MOTHER AND FATHER . . .

YOUR MOTHER AND FATHER WERE **KING** AND **QUEEN** OF **ATHEIA**. AND I WAS **QUEEN** OF THE LAND BEFORE THEM.

AND YOU, **THORN HARVESTAR**, ARE HEIR TO THE THRONE, AND I WILL **NOT** LET ANYTHING HAPPEN TO YOU!

I THOUGHT WE COULD KEEP YOU SAFE. LIVE OUT OUR DAYS HERE . . . RAISING THE COWS, FARMING A LITTLE PLOT OF LAND.

BUT IF THE LOCUSTS ARE BACK, THEN WAR IS UNAVOIDABLE . . .

. . . AND I HAVE FAILED.

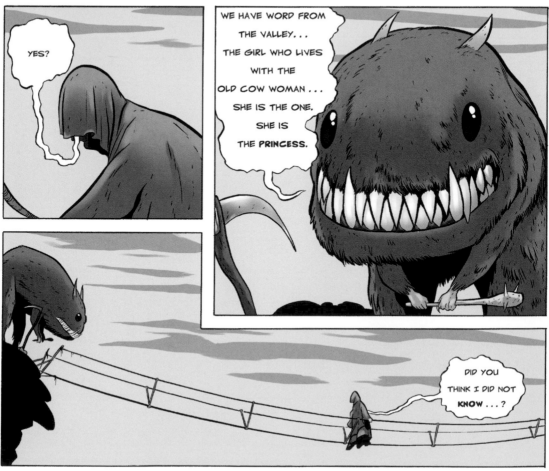

MENDING FENCES

... MASTER?

... IF I WAITED ... FOR YOUR COWARDLY UNDERLINGS TO BRING ME INFORMATION ..... WE WOULD ALL GROW OLD LISTENING TO SILENCE .....

I SUSPECT THAT IF **YOU**, KINGDOK ... SHOWED **LESS FEAR** FOR THE RED DRAGON ... YOUR WARRIORS MIGHT FOLLOW YOUR EXAMPLE ...

NOW LEAVE ME ...

WHAT NEWS DO YOU BRING US?

WE HAVE OUR ARMY.

THE POPULATION OF THE CAMP IS NEARING TEN THOUSAND . . . MORE RECRUITS ARRIVE EACH MORNING . . .

THAT IS GOOD.

THERE IS SOMETHING ELSE YOU WISH TO ASK US ABOUT?

THE GIRL . . . HER DREAMS ARE LIKE A BEACON . . . AND YET I CANNOT REACH HER . . .

IS HER STRENGTH SO GREAT?

EVEN IN HER IGNORANCE, HER STRENGTH IS GREAT . . . BUT THERE IS SOMETHING MORE . . . AS I REACHED OUT TO HER . . . A NEW BEACON APPEARED . . .

THE RED DRAGON SEEKS TO BRING A PAWN INTO PLAY. DO NOT CONCERN YOURSELF.

WHAT NEWS DO YOU BRING US OF THE STAR-BEARER?

THE ONE WHO BEARS A STAR IS AGAIN WITH THE VILLAGERS . . . IF IT IS YOUR DESIRE . . . WE WILL ATTACK THE TOWN.

AWAIT OUR INSTRUCTIONS.

MY LORD . . . THE RED DRAGON IS DANGEROUS. SHOULD WE NOT PREPARE - -

ASK NO MORE QUESTIONS.

...... BUT WHAT OF THIS
NEW **LIGHT** IN
THE **DREAMING** ...... ?

DO WE NOT ....
IGNORE THIS AT OUR
PERIL?

I KNOW HOW YOU FELLAS FEEL ABOUT THESE **BONE BOYS** . . .

. . . YOU WANNA **KILL 'EM** FOR MESSIN' WITH **TH' COW RACE!**

RRR!

GRR!

GRR!

RRRR!

RRR!

RRR!

WELL, **SO DO I,** BUT THEY OWE ME A **LOTTA EGGS,** AN' SO THEY GOTTA STAY **RIGHT HERE** AN' WORK IT OFF!

THAT MEANS I DON'T WANT **NO TROUBLE** FROM YOU GUYS. YOU GOT ME?

WHY NOT, LUCIUS? THEY GOTTA **PAY** FOR WHAT THEY DID!

I SAY WE TEAR THEIR LEGS OFF!

YEAH!

THEY TRIED TO MAKE **FOOLS** OUTTA US!

YOU MADE **FOOLS** OUTTA **YERSELVES!**

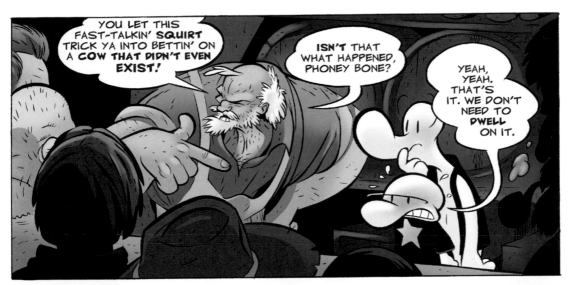

... NOW, THIS **CONTEST** I WAS TELLIN' YOU ABOUT -- IT'S BETWEEN ME AN' MISTER **PHONEY BONE** HERE. HE THINKS HE CAN RUN THIS JOINT **BETTER** THAN **I** CAN! WE'RE GONNA LET **YOU** DECIDE!

FROM NOW ON, THIS BAR WILL BE DIVIDED IN **TWO**! I'LL RUN **THIS** END, AN' TH' **BONES**'LL RUN **THAT** END.

HERE'S TH' **RULES**: YOU CAN TAKE YER BUSINESS TO WHICHEVER END OF TH' BAR YOU **WANT**! AFTER **ONE** MOON, THE END THAT EARNS TH' **MOST EGGS** FOR TH' TAVERN **WINS**!!

YOU CAN EITHER VOTE FOR **ME**, OR YOU CAN VOTE FOR **PHONEY**!

EVERYBODY UNDERSTAND TH' RULES?

GOOD!

WHO WANTS A DRINK?

WHAT ARE WE GONNA DO, PHONEY? NOBODY'S GONNA ORDER ANYTHING FROM **US!** IF WE LOSE THIS CONTEST WE'RE GONNA BE WASHIN' **DISHES** FOR TH' REST OF OUR **LIVES!**

I KNOW, I KNOW. THIS WASN'T ONE OF TH' **SMARTEST** BETS I'VE EVER MADE.

BUT WE'LL THINK OF **SOMETHIN'**, RIGHT? WE ALWAYS **DO!**

SURE! ALL WE GOTTA DO IS COME UP WITH SOME WAY TO **LURE** TH' TOWNSPEOPLE BACK DOWN TO **OUR** END. HOW HARD CAN **THAT** BE?

RIGHT! I'M **ON** IT! WE'LL HOLD A **LECTURE SERIES!** NO, WAIT! WE'LL USE **PUPPETS!** REALLY **CUTE** PUPPETS WITH HIGH, **SQUEAKY VOICES!**

GROAN

WE'RE DEAD.

GRAN'MA BEN?

THORN - -

... UM ...
I MEAN,
PRINCESS - -

DON'T
CALL
ME
THAT.

SORRY.

ALL THOSE DREAMS . . .
THEY WERE REAL.

DREAMS

THOSE DREAMS WERE **MEMORIES** OF THINGS THAT **REALLY HAPPENED** TO ME.

SOMETHING LIKE THAT.

THEY WERE JUST LIKE YOU SAID...

IN MY DREAMS I WAS TAKEN OUT OF A BURNING PALACE AS A LITTLE GIRL...

...AND IN THE DARK OF NIGHT, I WAS BROUGHT OVER THE MOUNTAINS TO THE DRAGONS' CAVE...

I EVEN DREAMED ABOUT THE **AMBUSH** ON THE DRAGON'S STAIR! I **DREAMED** ABOUT THE **MURDER OF MY PARENTS** AND I DIDN'T EVEN **KNOW** IT!

HOW CAN THIS BE?! HOW CAN I **DREAM** ABOUT THINGS THAT HAPPENED TO ME, BUT NOT **REMEMBER** THEM HAPPENING?!

SOMETIMES DREAMS KNOW MORE THAN WE DO.

MAYBE THERE'S MORE WE COULD LEARN . . .

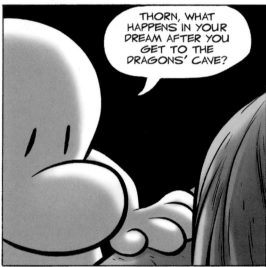

THORN, WHAT HAPPENS IN YOUR DREAM AFTER YOU GET TO THE DRAGONS' CAVE?

THE DRAGONS TAKE ME ON A LONG, LONG JOURNEY . . . UNDERGROUND.

WE GO TO A SPECIAL CHAMBER. IT'S VERY DARK AT FIRST . . .

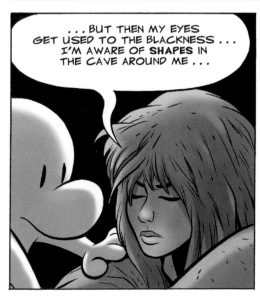

. . . BUT THEN MY EYES GET USED TO THE BLACKNESS . . . I'M AWARE OF **SHAPES** IN THE CAVE AROUND ME . . .

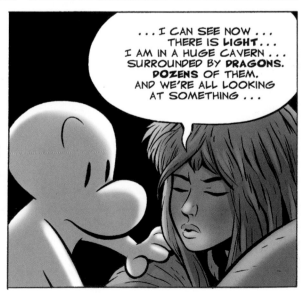

. . . I CAN SEE NOW . . . THERE IS **LIGHT** . . . I AM IN A HUGE CAVERN . . . SURROUNDED BY **DRAGONS**. **DOZENS** OF THEM. AND WE'RE ALL LOOKING AT SOMETHING . . .

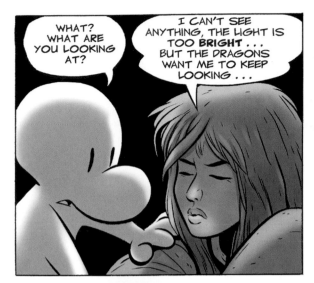

WHAT? WHAT ARE YOU LOOKING AT?

I CAN'T SEE ANYTHING, THE LIGHT IS TOO **BRIGHT** . . . BUT THE DRAGONS WANT ME TO KEEP LOOKING . . .

I THINK THE DRAGONS SEE SOMETHING, BUT I DON'T. IT'S TOO BRIGHT.

WHAT ELSE?

AFTER THAT I STAYED WITH THE DRAGONS. BUT I NEVER SAW THAT CHAMBER AGAIN . . .

WHAT ABOUT THE **GARDEN**? DON'T YOU WANT TO TELL GRAN'MA BEN ABOUT **THAT**?

SHE HEARD IT. SHE WAS **LISTENING IN** ON OUR CONVERSATION OUT IN THE **BARN**.

YES, I HEARD YOU.

I CAN'T BELIEVE IT . . . ALL THESE YEARS OF HIDING FOR **NOTHING**.

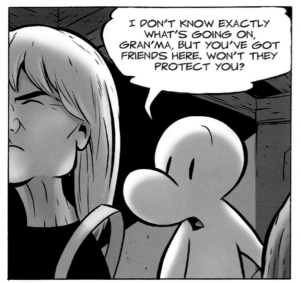

I DON'T KNOW EXACTLY WHAT'S GOING ON, GRAN'MA, BUT YOU'VE GOT FRIENDS HERE. WON'T THEY PROTECT YOU?

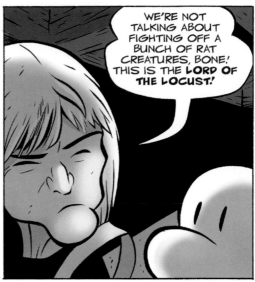

WE'RE NOT TALKING ABOUT FIGHTING OFF A BUNCH OF RAT CREATURES, BONE! THIS IS THE **LORD OF THE LOCUST!**

AN ENEMY MORE DANGEROUS THAN A **LEGION** OF RAT CREATURES.

THE LOCUST IS AN ANCIENT SPIRIT BURIED DEEP IN THE EARTH, BUT EVEN SO, HE CAN BEND PEOPLE TO HIS WILL.

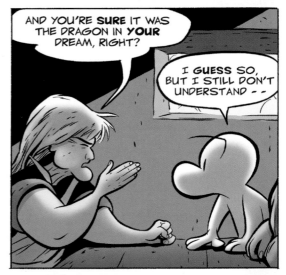

AND YOU'RE **SURE** IT WAS THE DRAGON IN **YOUR** DREAM, RIGHT?

I **GUESS** SO, BUT I STILL DON'T UNDERSTAND - -

MMMM. HE'S DOING THIS ON **PURPOSE!**

WHAT? WHAT'S HE DOING?

BEING IN MY DREAM? I DON'T GET IT.

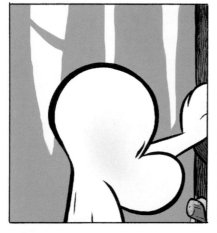

WELL, WELL, WELL, WELL . . . LOOK WHAT **SLITHERED** UP! READY TO CALL IT **QUITS**, SMART-GUY?

I ADMIT THIS MIGHT BE A LITTLE TOUGHER THAN I THOUGHT.

YOU'RE **WELCOME** TO HANG AROUND **THIS** END. YOU **MIGHT** LEARN SOMETHIN' ABOUT RUNNIN' A **BUSINESS** HERE ON TH' **WINNING** END OF TH' BAR!

DON'T GET **SMUG!** IT AIN'T OVER YET!

HEY -- WHAT'S EVERYBODY **DOIN'**?

HUH? HEY!

HEY!

WHERE'S EVERYBODY **GOIN'**?

WHAT TH'? WHAT'S GOIN' ON?

HOLY COW!

LOOKS LIKE TH' TABLES HAVE BEEN **TURNED**, PAL!

EXCUSE ME WHILE I GET **BACK** TO TH' **WINNING** END OF TH' BAR!

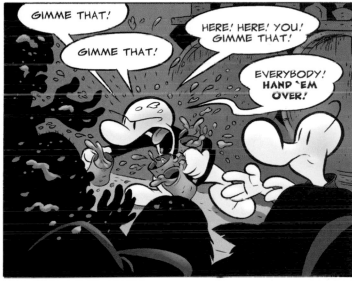

CHAPTER EIGHT

I -- I -- UH -- I JUST SAID I WISH FONE BONE'S **DRAGON** WAS HERE . . .

GASP!

GASP!

FONE BONE HAS A DRAGON?

GASP!

I DON'T BELIEVE IT.

WHO'S FONE BONE?

HE'S THAT **OTHER** BONE! THEIR **COUSIN!**

YEAH, RIGHT . . .

TH' ONE WHO'S ALWAYS HANGIN' AROUND WITH **THORN!**

SO WHERE IS THIS COUSIN OF YOURS **NOW?**

YEAH! AN' WHERE'S THE DRAGON?!

ALL RIGHT, **THAT'S ENOUGH!**

QUIT CROWDIN' TH' BAR!

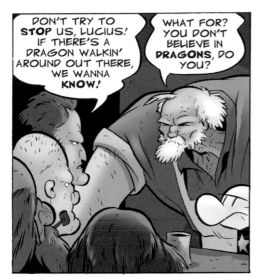

DON'T TRY TO **STOP** US, LUCIUS! IF THERE'S A **DRAGON** WALKIN' AROUND OUT THERE, WE WANNA **KNOW!**

WHAT FOR? YOU DON'T BELIEVE IN **DRAGONS**, DO YOU?

I DIDN'T SAY I **BELIEVED** IN 'EM . . . BUT THERE **HAVE** BEEN SOME PRETTY STRANGE **THINGS** GOIN' ON HERE LATELY!

STRANGE ENOUGH TO MAKE YOU START BELIEVIN' IN **CHILDREN'S STORIES?**

I KNOW IT SOUNDS **CRAZY**, BUT PEOPLE BEEN SEEIN' **STRANGE THINGS** IN TH' **WOODS** AT NIGHT! FOLKS ARE AFRAID TO GO **OUT!**

IT'S **TRUE!**

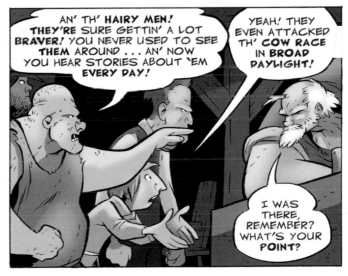

AN' TH' **HAIRY MEN!** THEY'RE SURE GETTIN' A LOT **BRAVER!** YOU NEVER USED TO SEE **THEM** AROUND . . . AN' NOW YOU HEAR STORIES ABOUT 'EM **EVERY DAY!**

YEAH! THEY EVEN ATTACKED TH' **COW RACE** IN **BROAD DAYLIGHT!**

I WAS THERE, REMEMBER? WHAT'S YOUR **POINT?**

IT **ALL** STARTED JUST ABOUT TH' SAME TIME **THESE** TWO SHOWED UP!

EVERYTHING WAS **FINE** UNTIL TH' **BONES** CAME TO OUR PART OF TH' **VALLEY!**

NOW ALL WE GOT IS **TROUBLE!**

LOOK HERE, BUB, I DON'T KNOW **WHOSE** DRAGON THIS IS, BUT IT **AIN'T OURS!** TH' **ONLY** DRAGON **I'VE** SEEN IS A BIG, LAZY **ORANGE** ONE, AN' HE WAS ALREADY **HERE!**

I GOT **NEWS** FOR YA, GASPING-BOY! YOU GOT A **LOTTA** WEIRD STUFF IN THIS **CRAZY** VALLEY, SO DON'T GO BLAMIN' **US** FOR YOUR **DRAGON** PROBLEMS!

BIG AN' **ORANGE!** THEN IT'S **TRUE!**

WHAT'S **TRUE?** YOU'RE NOT GONNA BELIEVE ANYTHING **PHONEY BONE** TELLS YOU, ARE YA? YOU CAN'T TRUST **THIS** RUNT AS FAR AS YOU CAN **THROW** HIM!

HE'S TELLIN' TH' **TRUTH,** LUCIUS! WE GOT US A **REAL, LIVE DRAGON** WALKIN' AROUND OUT THERE!

YOU TAKE TH' **CAKE,** WENDELL, YOU KNOW THAT?

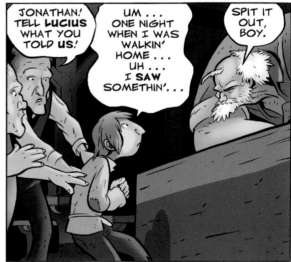

JONATHAN! TELL **LUCIUS** WHAT YOU **TOLD US!**

UM . . . ONE NIGHT WHEN I WAS WALKIN' HOME . . . UH . . . I **SAW** SOMETHIN'. . .

SPIT IT OUT, BOY.

THERE WASN'T HARDLY ANY **MOON** OUT, SO IT WAS KINDA DARK. AN' REAL **QUIET.** THEN I **SAW** IT. A HUGE SHAPE MOVIN' BETWEEN TH' **TREES!** IT WAS BIG AND IT WAS **ORANGE** -- AND WHEN IT WAS GONE, ALL THAT WAS LEFT WAS TH' SMELL OF **BRIMSTONE!**

THERE, SEE? WHAT DO YOU SAY TO **THAT,** LUCIUS? STILL THINK DRAGONS ARE JUST **CHILDREN'S STORIES?**

AAH! I AIN'T GOT **NOTHIN'** TO SAY. . .

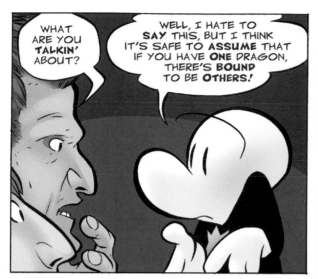

WHAT TH' HELL DO YOU THINK YOU'RE DOIN'?

YOU KNOW THIS LITTLE **BET** YOU AN' I GOT GOIN' TO SEE WHO CAN SELL TH' MOST BEER?

YEAH?

I'M ABOUT TO WIN!

SMILEY! START POURIN'!

NOTHIN' LIKE A LITTLE ALCOHOL TO GREASE TH' WHEELS OF MOB MENTALITY! RIGHT, BOYS?!

RIGHT! YAY!

THE FIRST ROUND'S ON ME! BUT AFTER **THAT**, YOU GOTTA PAY!

THAT'S IT!

THREE CHEERS FOR PHONEY!

WELCOME, STRANGER. CAN I **HELP** YOU? YOU NEED A **ROOM**, OR JUST LOOKIN' TO SLAKE YOUR **THIRST?**

I BRING NEWS FROM THE SOUTH.

WAIT FOR ME OUTSIDE.

HEY THERE, FONE BONE! HOW YOU DOIN' THESE **FINE** DAYS?

HELLO, TED! I'M DOIN' OKAY . . . **THORN** AN' **GRAN'MA BEN** COULD BE BETTER . . .

HOW ABOUT YOU?

GOOD! JUST BEEN TA SEE **LUCIUS** AN' YER **COUSINS!**

OH, YEAH? HOW ARE THEY? ARE THEY CAUSIN' ANY TROUBLE?

THEY'S KICKIN' UP SOME DUST, **YOU** KNOW, JES' LIKE THEY DO. BUT WHAT'S ALL THIS YOU SAYIN' 'BOUTS **GRAN'MA** AN' **THORNY?** SOMETHIN' **WRONG?**

WELL, **THORN** IS OUT IN TH' **BARN** LAYIN' FACEDOWN IN TH' **HAY.** SHE'S PRETTY **UPSET.** SHE GOT SOME **BAD NEWS** ABOUT HER **PARENTS,** AN' SOME OTHER STUFF ABOUT HER **PAST** . . .

LIKE **WHAT?**

OH, UH, I PROBABLY SHOULDN'T **SAY**, TED. I MEAN, I **TRUST** YOU, BUT I THINK THEY'RE KINDA **SECRET** --

SHE FIND OUT HER FOLKS WAS KILLED BY **RAT CREATURES**?

OH, BOY. GRAN'MA **TOLD** HER, HUH? SO I SUPPOSE SHE KNOWS HER **REAL** LAST NAME IS **HARVESTAR** . . . THA'S A **ROYAL** NAME, Y'KNOW.

UM, YEAH. SHE **KNOWS**. GRAN'MA TOLD HER.

THORN HARVESTAR. **CROWN PRINCESS** OF TH' WHOLE **SHOOTIN' MATCH!** BIG STUFF, BIG STUFF.

HOW DID YOU **KNOW** THAT? **THORN** DIDN'T EVEN KNOW!

BUGS KNOW A **LOTTA** STUFF FOLKS WOULDN'T S'POSE THEY'D KNOW.

SAY, THAT **REMINDS** ME, I GOT AN IMPORTANT **MESSAGE** FROM **LUCIUS** FOR **GRAN'MA BEN!** WHERE **IS** SHE?

SHE WAS IN TH' **HOUSE** LAST I SAW HER.

OKEE DOKEE, BONE! CATCH YA **LATER**, BYE!

BYE!

HEY, BONE! GO GRAB YOUR KNAPSACK AN' MEET ME IN TH' BARN! **NOW!**

YES, MA'AM!

GRAN'MA – – ?

WE HAVE TO LEAVE.

HERE'S YOUR BEDROLL AND A FEW OF YOUR PERSONAL THINGS . . .

C'MON IN HERE, BONE.

ACCORDING TO MY SOURCES, SOMEONE IS GATHERING AN ARMY IN THE EASTERN MOUNTAINS AND THAT PERSON IS WEARING A **HOOD.**

IF IT'S THE **SAME** HOODED FIGURE FROM THORN'S DREAMS, THEN THE RAT CREATURES KNOW WHO WE ARE.

THERE'S MORE BAD NEWS . . .

IT SEEMS LARGE NUMBERS OF **RAT CREATURES** ARE HEADING THIS WAY.

THINGS THAT GO BUMP IN THE NIGHT

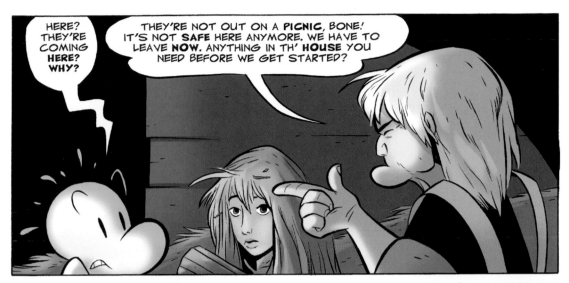

HERE? THEY'RE COMING **HERE?** WHY?

THEY'RE NOT OUT ON A **PICNIC**, BONE! IT'S NOT **SAFE** HERE ANYMORE. WE HAVE TO LEAVE **NOW.** ANYTHING IN TH' **HOUSE** YOU NEED BEFORE WE GET STARTED?

I -- MIGHT NEED SOMETHING **WARMER** TO WEAR . . .

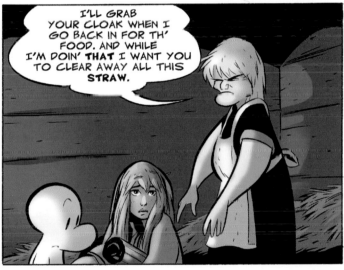

I'LL GRAB YOUR CLOAK WHEN I GO BACK IN FOR TH' FOOD. AND WHILE I'M DOIN' **THAT** I WANT YOU TO CLEAR AWAY ALL THIS **STRAW.**

THERE'S A SECRET DOOR UNDER THERE, AN' INSIDE IS AN OLD TRUNK. **HAUL** IT OUTTA THERE AN' I'LL BE RIGHT BACK!

YOU GOT IT?
GOOD!

OKAY, STEP BACK.

WHAT ARE **YOU** LOOKIN' AT? I USED TO WEAR THIS THING ALL TH' **TIME!**

ALL RIGHT, **LOAD UP!** AN' MAKE SURE YOUR PACKS ARE TIED DOWN GOOD AN' **TIGHT!** WE GOT A LONG WALK AHEAD OF US!

THAT'S IT? WE'RE JUST GONNA **LEAVE?!**

THAT'S IT.

YOU'VE BEEN AWFUL **QUIET,** THORN. YOU GONNA BE OKAY?

I'M FINE IF **YOU** ARE.

...TO BE CONTINUED.

About JEFF SMITH

JEFF SMITH was born and raised in the American Midwest and learned about cartooning from comic strips, comic books, and watching animated shorts on TV. After four years of drawing comic strips for The Ohio State University's student newspaper and co-founding Character Builders animation studio in 1986, Smith launched the comic book *BONE* in 1991. Between *BONE* and other comics projects, Smith spends much of his time on the international guest circuit promoting comics and the art of graphic novels.

More about BONE

An instant classic when it first appeared in the U.S. as an underground comic book in 1991, *BONE* has since garnered 38 international awards and sold a million copies in 15 languages. Now, Scholastic's GRAPHIX imprint is publishing full-color graphic novel editions of the nine-book *BONE* series.